TRYST

(a *Take It Off* novel)

Sometimes all a girl needs is a little fling…

Talie Ronson needs a vacation.

From life.

Since she caught her cheating, loser husband in bed with his assistant, her life has been on a steady spiral—right into hell. Her car's a junker, her job sucks, and her perfect, gorgeous sister likes to brag about her wonderful life every time they "do" lunch.

In an effort to salvage what's left of her life and her sanity, she takes the advice of her kooky best friend and takes off to Topsail Island. A week at the beach, alone, is exactly what she needs to recharge, regroup, and relax.

Only, her alone time is about to get derailed.

Gavin Palmer's favorite activity is walking around in his boxers and eating junk food. He and his neighbors have an understanding. They stay out of his business and he stays out of theirs. He lives at the beach, not for vacation, but for isolation. He's had enough of people to last him a lifetime.

Gavin's isolation is interrupted when his normally quiet neighbor starts disturbing his peace. He stomps across the sand to give the guy a piece of his mind... only it isn't a guy.

It's Talie.

She's maddening, nosy, and talks too much.

But she's hot and her bedroom eyes have him thinking maybe he's had enough solitude. Maybe a week of company is exactly what he needs.

Maybe what they both need is a no-strings-attached tryst.

Praise for the **Take It Off** series

"I love all of Cambria's books, but Torch *is one if my favorites by her so far. Holt and Katie have chemistry like no other. There was a perfect mixture of steam, passion, and romance."*
—*New York Times* and *USA Today* bestselling author
Shanora Williams for *TORCH*

"Cam was so swoon-worthy. He was everything I look for in a book boyfriend. He was hot, sexy, had a little bad boy edge, but he was also protective and loving. The mystery was also a great element. It kept me flipping the pages quickly to figure it out. And when it was revealed, it was shocking."
—Bestselling author Amber Garza for *TEASE*

"All hail the new queen of HOT romance! My new favorite romance of the last year. I adore this book. Nash & Ava… such a great story. I think I may have a new book boyfriend. This is a true romance story, but it mixes in danger, deception, & desire."
—Author Kieran Thorne for *TEMPT*

"TEXT kept me up late turning pages. When I wasn't reading it, I was thinking about it. With lovable characters and a tight suspense plot, this is a great weekend read!"
—Bestselling author Ella James for *TEXT*

TRYST

Take It Off Series

CAMBRIA HEBERT

Published by: Cambria Hebert Books, LLC

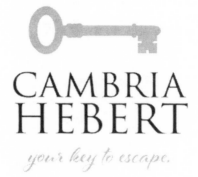

CAMBRIA
HEBERT

your key to escape.

http://www.cambriahebert.com

Interior design and typesetting by Sharon Kay
Cover design by MAE I DESIGN
Edited by Cassie McCown
Copyright 2014 by Cambria Hebert
ISBN: 978-1-938857-46-1

Other Book by Cambria Hebert

Heven and Hell Series

Before
Masquerade
Between
Charade
Bewitched
Tirade
Beneath
Renegade
Heven & Hell Anthology

Death Escorts

Recalled
Charmed

Take It Off

Torch
Tease
Tempt
Text
Tipsy
Tricks
Tattoo

DEDICATION

To every girl (or guy!) who's ever had a tryst.

TRYST

PROLOGUE

Talie

I hadn't had sex in six months. *Six months.* I was practically a born-again virgin. I mean, seriously. They say when you get married, your sex life goes down the toilet, but I didn't know who "they" were, and I thought for sure my sex life wouldn't go downhill until I was some old lady.

I was not old.

And I kind of wanted to punch "they" in the face.

I'll blame my aggression on sexual frustration.

Weren't men supposed to be a bunch of horn-dogs? In my experience, they sure were. My husband and I used to have sex all the time, but it slowly began to dwindle and then it pretty much fell off the face of the earth.

But that was going to change. I was going to do something about it. The way I saw it, I could let my insides shrivel up from lack of pleasure, or I could take the bull by the horns (or penis).

Shriveling up didn't sound so appealing so I took the afternoon off from work (no loss there) and decided to go home and set the stage for a night of getting it on. On my way, I stopped at the store and picked up some candles, a see-through hot-pink nightie, and some edible massage oil.

I let myself into the apartment and shut the door behind me. Just as I made it to the kitchen counter, I heard a sound.

A moan.

I set the bag on the counter, soundlessly, and cocked my head, listening. Another moan floated through the apartment, and I wrinkled my nose.

Had I left the TV on when I left for work this morning?

And if so, what the hell kind of daytime shows did they play these days?

I padded down the hallway, over the plush carpet, and stopped in front of my partially closed bedroom door.

The sounds of heavy breathing and the bouncing of a mattress were unmistakable.

I was really trying not to think bad thoughts.

Really.

But I mean... it smelled like sex out here. A deep, musky scent that clung to the air.

I laid my palm against the door and pushed it open, stepping slowly in the doorway.

It took me quite a few seconds to register what I was seeing. Shock rendered me motionless. All I could do was stand there and gape.

I hadn't left the TV on this morning.

And now I knew why my husband hadn't pleased me in the past six months.

He was too busy pleasing someone else. Someone who was *not* his wife.

They were so involved in the act that they didn't even know I was there. So I watched them. This was my house. That was my bed. And frankly, a part of me thought I was dreaming.

The white combed-cotton sheets that I had shopped for diligently where all wound around the legs of the couple in the center of the king-sized bed. The pillows I lovingly picked out were all skewed from the thrusting and movement going on, and the dark-gray comforter was half falling off the bed and onto the floor.

There was a woman sitting on top of my husband. Her hair was very long and thick, the color of chestnuts, and it waved down her back wildly like they'd been at the deed for a while already. As I stared, she pushed up off him and sat up, titling her head back and letting out a very loud moan as she moved over him, grinding her body against his.

I watched as my husband reached up and grabbed her breasts, giving them a little squeeze and grunting with pleasure.

Pain sliced through my belly.

How could he do this to me? How could he tell me he loved me, ask me to spend the rest of my life with him, and then bring another woman home and into our bed?

The pain I felt might have been incapacitating, but it didn't stay long enough. It was quickly replaced by anger. Hot, furious sparks ignited inside me and my feet began to move.

I walked farther into the room and stopped at the edge of the bed.

"Talie!" My husband gasped, shooting into a sitting position. The woman screwing my husband didn't slide off of him. Instead, she buried her face into his naked chest, like she was trying to hide.

It pissed me off.

I reached out and grabbed a handful of that thick, luxurious hair and yanked her backward. "Get the hell off my husband, you dirty ho."

She screeched as I pulled her back off his lap, revealing his proud member. I scowled and dumped her and her fake boobs on the floor.

"Talie, I can explain," he said, pulling the blanket up to cover his manhood. He was probably nervous I might grab it like I grabbed Barbie's hair.

I wasn't touching that thing ever again.

And really… was that like every idiot's favorite line? *I can explain.*

"You don't need to explain. My eyes work just fine," I snapped.

The girl scrambled up off the carpet and started gathering her clothes, which were tossed around my bedroom.

"I hope he satisfies you because he sure as hell never satisfied me," I spat.

Her eyes widened and Blake (my cheating husband) began to sputter.

"Shut up," I told him as I grabbed Barbie again and started towing her through the apartment toward the front door.

"I'm not dressed!" she screeched.

"What a shame."

I flung open the door and shoved her out. She stood there in the center of the hallway, clutching her clothes against her naked chest. Her eyes narrowed and a mean look crossed her face.

"He told me you never made him happy."

"You might wanna pay a visit to the surgeon who did your tits. They're lopsided." I slammed the door in her shocked face.

My chest was heaving and my hands were shaking when I turned around.

Blake was standing there, buttoning up a pair of black slacks. "Was that really necessary?"

At least he didn't try to come up with some stupid-ass excuse. There was no excuse for him. And there was no excuse for why I married him, why I stayed in a marriage that was clearly never going to make me happy.

I opened the door once more. Thankfully, Barbie had already run off.

"Get out."

He stared at me.

"I'm pretty sure I didn't stutter. I said get the hell out."

"This is my apartment too," he said, crossing his arms over his chest.

"Oh, you can have it," I replied calmly. "I'll be gone in two hours."

His arms dropped to his sides. "Where are you going to go?" Shock registered on his face, and I realized then that he didn't respect me. He probably never did. He knew he would get caught eventually, but he thought I would stay. He thought I would put up with it.

He didn't know me at all.

"It's none of your business. Now get out before I start to scream."

He came forward, stopping just in front of me. He reached up as if he were going to touch my face. I slapped his hand away. "I'll be gone in two hours."

Once he was in the hall, I slammed the door and threw the locks. I sagged against the white-painted wood and expelled a breath. I felt like I just ran a marathon. My chest squeezed tight, my stomach hurt, and every single limb on my body was heavy and exhausted.

Tears threatened behind my eyes and I sniffled. I glanced at the bag full of my romance supplies.

What a big, fat freaking joke.

I shoved away from the door, lifted my chin, and dashed away the unshed tears.

I could feel sorry for myself later.

Right now, I had to pack.

1

Talie

I went to the closest bank and transferred all the money out of our joint accounts and into my personal savings.

Okay, not all of our money.

I left him a dollar.

I thought that was very generous.

After I put some cash in my wallet, I drove across town to a gated neighborhood. If it wasn't for the permanent pass I carried, I knew the guard would never let me behind the gate. The car I drove didn't belong in a neighborhood like this. It was a clunker.

We always planned to buy me a new one. We were saving up because Blake bought a BMW right before we got married and we didn't want to take on another payment so early in our marriage.

He was a complete douche.

My sister opened the door to her three thousand-square-foot house in the burbs, looking like she just stepped off a runway in Paris.

Yep, she was one of *those* women.

The kind of woman who never had a hair out of place. The kind who woke up in the morning looking like some kind of divine angel, with perfectly tousled hair and glowing skin. She always dressed perfectly, even if it was lounge clothes. Her long, dark hair was always curled, always shining, and her face was always perfectly made up.

She was a true southern belle.

I looked like the Hunchback of Notre Dame next to her.

"Talie!" she said, her voice breathless (it was always breathless). "I wasn't expecting you! Did we have a lunch date I forgot about?"

I wanted to laugh. She never forgot any date she made. "Sorry to just show up, Joanna. Is now a bad time?"

"No, come in," she said, holding the door wide so I could step into her entryway with cherry hardwood floors and soaring ceilings. "I just finished up my work for the day."

My sister worked from home as an accountant. She only worked part time because she had two young children, and really, they didn't need the money. I always just thought her decision to keep a few clients even after she had children was more because she liked telling people she was an accountant.

"Where are the twins?" I asked, looking around for Ainsley and Avery. They were two-year-old twin girls, the spitting image of their mother.

"Tiffany took them to the pool."

Tiffany was the girls' nanny and the pool was part of the amenities that came with the neighborhood.

"Would you like something to drink?" Joanna asked as I followed her through the house and stepped into the large, open kitchen. It had cream-colored custom cabinetry, a glass-tiled backsplash, and quartz countertops.

"No thanks," I said. What I really wanted was an entire bottle of wine. And a straw.

Joanna opened up the massive stainless-steel fridge and pulled out a glass pitcher filled with water. Floating in the water were thick slices of red apple and many cinnamon sticks. She drank that water concoction every day and claimed it helped keep her figure so trim.

I secretly wondered if she ever ate.

Yeah. That was bitter. In my own defense, I just caught my loser soon-to-be ex-husband in bed with a woman who spent time under the knife to look like Barbie.

I sighed and watched Joanna pour herself a glass of the water. I shouldn't have come here so soon. I knew better. On a good day, I only found my sister and all her perfect glory mildly annoying. On a bad day, I wondered what the hell I did to deserve the leftovers from my parent's gene pool. On a day like today...

On a day like today, I found myself thinking I should have just forgot to put my junker of a car in park and then got out to let it "accidentally" run me over.

Of course, I would never actually do something like that.

That was just hella dramatic.

Well, that and the fact that I would be the one person who would get run over by her scrap metal on wheels and survive… only to live with the mangled mess of my body.

"So what brings you by?" Joanna asked, perching on the edge of her upholstered chairs at the round glass table nearby.

"I need Jack's help."

Jack was Joanna's husband. He was a successful lawyer here in Raleigh and had his eyes set on a partnership at one of the biggest firms in town. I had no doubt he would get it. If he wasn't my brother-in-law, I wouldn't be able to afford thirty minutes of his time.

Good thing for family discounts.

Joanna's delicately shaped brows rose. "Whatever do you need a lawyer for?"

"I'm filing for divorce." The words were practically a grenade that dropped into the center of the room and obliterated the calm, quiet atmosphere that was my sister's kitchen.

She gasped and put a hand to her chest. "A divorce!" she said like it was some foreign term. "Why in the world would you be doing that?"

"I caught Blake in bed this afternoon. In my bed. With his secretary."

Joanna thought for a moment. "There has to be a reasonable explanation, Talie."

"They were naked. She was on top of him."

Her lips formed a little O.

"He's cheating on me. Probably has been for a long time."

"Now, you don't know that for sure. Perhaps it was a one-time thing. A mistake."

Sometimes a woman didn't have to know something to *know* it.

And I *knew* Blake had sex with lopsided boob Barbie more than once.

"Oh, it was a mistake all right," I muttered. "A mistake that I married him."

"Talie!" Joanna admonished. Her tone set my back teeth on edge. She set her apple cinnamon water aside and stood, placing her pink-manicured fingers on her hips. "Blake is a good man. He's very successful; he's good looking, comes from a strong family with roots deep in the southern soil. He's quite the catch."

And this is why I knew better than to come here. "Are you actually defending the fact he was sleeping with another woman. In my bed?"

She blanched like the image left a distasteful flavor in her mouth. "What I'm saying is you took vows. You can't throw away a good marriage so rashly."

Good marriage. Rash. Vows.

Suddenly I felt extremely sick to my stomach.

I stood up, ignoring the dizziness that swept through my foggy brain. "What time will Jack be home tonight?"

"Probably about seven."

"Can you please ask him to draw up the divorce papers? Tell him I'll come by later this week to sign them all and set things in motion."

"Where are you going?"

"To Claire's place. I'm staying there." At least, I prayed she would let me when I flung myself on the couch and begged to stay.

"You need to go home. Work things out—"

I cut her off. "I can't talk about this right now."

"Yes. Well, I'm sure you've had a trying day."

Yes. Trying.

I was *trying* to understand how the hell this happened. How could I have been so wrong about the man I married? I was also *trying* not to be pissed off my sister was kind of taking his side.

"Why don't you stay? We can have tea and talk this over calmly."

Calmly = Joanna telling me what to do.

"Thanks for the offer, sis," I said, already heading toward the front door. "But I can't, not right now. You'll call Jack and ask him to bring the papers?"

"Of course, but are you sure you don't want to think about it?"

I couldn't *not* think about it. "I'm sure."

Joanna's face was drawn into a frown, creating a crease between her perfectly arched brows. I sighed, reached out, and hugged her. She returned the embrace, and I felt tears prick the back of my eyes. I pulled away, opening the door.

"Thanks, Jo-Jo," I said, using the name I called her when we were kids.

I didn't look back when the door closed behind me, but I did let out a long breath. I loved my sister, but sometimes I wanted to strangle her.

Of course, it was just my luck that when I turned the key in my ancient VW Jetta that the engine sounded like an old man about to cough up his lung. I smacked the steering wheel and let out a frustrated cry. "Today is not the day for this," I demanded of my car. "Work, dammit!

I turned the key again and this time the engine sputtered to life. I leaned my forehead against the steering wheel for a few moments, allowing myself seconds of self-pity before driving out of the ritzy neighborhood and toward my therapist's office.

The parking lot was packed when I got there, but I managed to snag the last spot around back. I guess I wasn't the only one in need of therapy today. The scent of fried dough wafted through the afternoon breeze, beckoning me closer and offering thousands of calories in comfort.

I didn't have to worry about calories anymore. Since no one was going to be seeing me in my panties, I could eat as many donuts as I wanted and not feel an ounce of guilt.

A woman holding a giant cup of iced coffee held the door as I stepped inside and stood at the end of the line.

My therapist = Dunkin Donuts.

What? Donuts make everyone feel better.

Inside the donut shop was a companion counter for Baskin Robbins. Donuts *and* ice cream? I couldn't possibly.

Oh, wait. Yes. Yes, I could.

I grabbed a round, white ice cream cake—that said "Congratulations!" on the top in pink icing—out of the freezer and stepped back in line. At the counter, I ordered a dozen donuts and one of those giant coffee rolls. And because my anxiety and stress meter was off the charts, I ordered a large brown sugar latte.

Coffee had the opposite effect on me than it seemed to have on others. It didn't make me jittery or keyed up. Coffee actually calmed me down.

Once all the sugar, carbs, and caffeine were piled in my arms, I climbed back in my car and checked my cell phone. It was still fairly early in the day, and I wasn't sure Claire would be home yet, so I dialed her number.

"Hey, girl," she chimed after two rings.

"Are you still at work?"

"Unfortunately," she intoned, sounding bored. Working as a manager at a large retail store must not be very entertaining. "Aren't you supposed to be too?"

"I left early."

"Lucky."

"So I'm gonna need somewhere to stay." Damn my suddenly wobbly voice.

There was a meaningful pause on the other end of the line. "You know where I keep the spare key."

I nodded and then told myself I was in idiot because she couldn't see me.

"Want me to get some donuts?" she asked.

"I already got some. I got an ice cream cake too."

"That bad, huh?" she said. She knew me so well.

"That bad." I confirmed.

"I feel an extreme headache coming on," she began. "Damn these headaches of mine. I'm going to have to leave early today." Her voice was heavily laced with *regret*.

I smiled.

"I'll see ya in a few," she said, and I could already hear papers on her desk being shoveled around.

"Thanks, Claire."

"Don't eat it all before I get there."

After I set down the phone, I glared at the dashboard. "I'm not in the mood for your hormonal activity today," I told the car. It must have known I meant business because it started on the first try.

I pulled out of the lot and took a good, long sip of the coffee and sighed.

2

Talie

Was it possible to have a junk food hangover?

Was it possible my therapist wasn't quite as helpful as it should be?

Yes, and yes.

Sunlight streamed between the edges of the white blinds in the living room, creating stripes of brightness across the floor and furniture. I cracked one eye open and took in my surroundings. It took a moment to place where I was.

Waking up somewhere other than my own bed, in my own home, was a little jarring. But, it wasn't like I was at a bar, got drunk, and went home with some guy whose name I didn't even know. The red sofa, purple patterned armchair, and array of colored pillows all over the place were very familiar.

I pushed up into a sitting position and leaned against the red fabric while I pushed a hand through my tangled, fine hair. Plastic forks and spoons littered the coffee table. The empty white cake box was dotted with crumbs from the crushed cookie layer that was in the center of the ice cream cake.

We ate the entire thing.

And just like that, everything that happened the day before came rushing over me.

Turns out feeling like a giant fatty whose blood sugar levels were likely going to put her in a coma wasn't as bad as reliving the moment you caught your husband being ridden by some bimbo in the center of your Pottery Barn sheets.

I spent all night drowning my sorrows in ice cream, donuts, and, by the looks of the empty cans on the table, soda. The inside of my mouth was coated with some sort of thick, sticky substance, and I made a face. It was probably congealed sugar...

I stood, ignoring the headache behind my eyes and the feeling I had a truckload of sand behind my lids. I bent sluggishly to lift my duffle bag off the floor and then shut myself in the bathroom, turning the shower as hot as it would go.

After peeling off the clothes I wore yesterday and then slept in, I dumped them into the nearby trash can. They were dirty. Dirty in the way no washing machine or bleach would clean. They would forever be the clothes in which I discovered the truth about my husband. If I ever wore them again, I would remember the exact sound of *them* moaning from the bedroom. I would remember that sudden drop of my belly when I walked into the bedroom and saw them...

I couldn't ever wear those clothes again.

The scalding spray of the water made me grimace as heat stung my skin. I didn't bother adjusting the temperature. My skin felt dirty too. I didn't know how long Blake had been sleeping around, but considering the fact we hadn't been intimate in six months, I knew it had to be at least that long. Maybe it was longer.

Maybe he'd never been faithful at all.

I shuddered. The thought of him putting himself inside me *and* someone else made me sick. I picked up the white bar of soap and began to scrub myself. I didn't stop until my skin felt raw and sore. Once I was done, I turned my attention to my hair. Even wet, it was a tangled mess. It was long, probably too long for its fine texture. But Joanna said long hair was more feminine. Joanna said men liked women with long, shining hair.

Blake always said he liked it when I wore my hair down around my shoulders.

Blake was a big liar.

After I worked out all the knots with shampoo and extra conditioner, I stood there under the spray, just watching the water circle around the drain before disappearing.

What now?

What did a twenty-four-year-old woman do when she learned her husband wasn't who she thought he was?

Joanna wanted me to stay with him. She made that perfectly clear yesterday. Claire thought I should make him miserable before taking him for everything he was worth.

That seemed like wasting a lot of energy on someone who really didn't deserve any more of my time. I always thought being married was the ultimate goal in life. To have someone who would always love

you, who would always be there. To build a family
and a home around that love.

It seemed like I spent most of my teenage years
daydreaming about how perfect life would be once I
met that one man meant for me.

How naïve I was.

Not anymore. No, now my naivety was washing
down the drain with my discarded shower water. The
water turned cool and I shut off the valves and
quickly dried off before wrapping the soft fabric
around myself. I pulled out my light tangle-free leave-
in conditioner, my wide-tooth comb, and my
volumizing mouse. After I applied all the product and
combed my locks, I felt utterly exhausted and
weighed down. I didn't want to face having to blow it
dry, so I twisted it up on my head in a sleek topknot.

My eyes were slightly puffy from crying last
night, so I pulled out a little wand of cooling eye
serum and applied it to the bags that so graciously
added themselves to my face. As I applied some
moisturizer to the rest of my skin, I let out a deep
sigh. The thought of going into work today literally
made me want to jab myself in the eye with a pencil.

But I was going to go.

I wasn't going to hide at Claire's like I was
ashamed. Like I'd done something wrong. This wasn't
my fault. Yeah, maybe I wasn't the easiest to live with.
And yeah, maybe I wasn't the sexiest or prettiest girl
around.

But I didn't deserve to be cheated on.

After dressing in a pair of black linen pants and a
black-and-white striped blouse, I left the bathroom in
a cloud of steam, and the scent of richly roasted
coffee wafted down the hallway toward me.

Claire was in the kitchen, dressed in an oversized T-shirt and black leggings. Her short red hair was tousled from sleep, but since she wore it like that on a daily basis, it already looked perfect.

"You roll out of bed practically ready for work," I grumped, helping myself to a huge-ass mug of joe. I didn't bother adding my usual creamer. Maybe if I drank it black, the strong brew would burn up some of the sugar still floating in my system.

"Well, aren't you Suzie Sunshine this morning," she quipped and eyed me. "How are you?"

Some of the coffee I just slurped dribbled down my chin, and I used the back of my free hand to wipe it away. "Peachy."

"You should take the day off. Hell, the rest of the week. Give yourself a break. It's not every day a woman finds her man—" She blanched and stopped speaking.

"I'm going to work, and he's not my man anymore."

"You're really going to do it?" she asked, helping herself to some coffee.

I told her about going to see Jack. I told her I was filing for divorce. She warned me not to make a rash decision that I might regret later. She told me I should take some time and really think about what I wanted.

The thing was, cheating was cheating. Today, tomorrow… five years from now, that wasn't going to change.

"I'm going to see Jack later today to get things in motion."

She nodded. "I figured as much. You know I support you, right?"

The short sentence made something in my chest tighten. "I know you do," I said, my voice softening. It was good to know that no matter what, Claire would always be in my corner.

The muffled ringing of my cell phone floated into the kitchen, interrupting our coffee and wallowing. I carried the half-empty mug into the living room where my bag was lying on the floor and reached in to pull out my phone. The screen flashed HOME across it as it rang.

A splinter of pain pierced my chest. That wasn't my home anymore.

I hit the IGNORE button and turned away. Claire lifted her eyebrow in silent inquiry as I returned to the kitchen. "Him?" she asked.

"Yep," I replied, drinking more coffee.

"He isn't going to just let you go," she said, voicing the exact thoughts that were occupying the back of my mind.

"He doesn't have a choice." I drained the rest of the coffee and placed the mug in the sink. Then I went to finish getting ready for work.

It was going to be a very long day.

3

Talie

Did I ever mention I loved my job?

No?

That's because it sucked.

My job was to do all the billing in a local doctor's office. I spent most of my day sitting behind a desk in my cramped little office, dealing with insurance companies, billing codes, and people who thought it was unfair their insurance didn't pay more for their bills.

A lot of times, I agreed with those people, but I wasn't allowed to say so. My job was to put up with their angry calls and then try to work out a system or payment plan so they could pay what they owed.

It also didn't help that the primary doctor in the office was an egotistical chauvinist. All the girls that worked in the office (there were no men) were all very beautiful, with toned bodies, perfect hair, and large chests.

And then there was me.

I did have full breasts, but my hair was never perfect and my body needed to spend about six months in the gym before it looked toned. I was one of those women who looked "soft." I was shaped like an hourglass with ample boobs and, what people fondly told me as I was growing up, a bubble butt.

How telling anyone their butt was large was supposed to be fond I had no idea.

While I wasn't really overweight I could stand to lose about ten pounds and to maybe run off some of the extra cushion in my trunk. Eating an entire ice cream cake and box of donuts was not the way to do this. I knew that, but I guess I didn't really care. I'd never been the pretty one or the one that caught the stares of men whenever I was out. People always told me I was *cute*. I was always the one everyone would be friends with while they lusted after my friends.

In high school, I used to wish just one guy would tell me I was beautiful, because being beautiful in one man's eyes would make being cute to everyone else okay.

I never did find that guy.

But then Blake came along in college. He was charming, charismatic, and self-confident. I was surprised when he started looking at me like I was more than just a friend. He could have any girl he wanted… so why was he looking at me?

I asked him that once, after we had a few dates. He said he liked a woman who wasn't so caught up in herself. A woman who didn't just think about how she looked all the time, someone who liked to laugh and eat popcorn with butter at movies. He also said he liked my laugh, that it was the laugh of an angel.

Angels = beautiful.

The memory left a bitter taste in my mouth. What he'd really meant was he wanted a woman who thought about him more than herself. A woman who would be too busy thinking how lucky she was to be with a successful businessman who had a well-respected family to notice he only cared about himself. He thought I would be too grateful to notice he lied. When he said he didn't want a woman caught up in herself, what he really meant was he wanted someone who would look the other way when he slept with the kind of woman I wasn't.

He should have paid better attention.

I might not be beautiful.

But I was nobody's doormat.

He called my phone again about an hour after I started working, so I just shut it off and tossed it in my desk drawer. I wasn't in the mood to deal with him today.

I was buried in numbers and paperwork when Dr. Asik walked by my office. I heard the high-pitched giggle of one of the girl's out front.

I rolled my eyes. I never flirted with him. I never smiled coyly and giggled when he complimented my outfit (not that he ever did). I often wondered how many of the girls he was sleeping with in this office, and while it always gave me the creeps, it never totally made me sick… until now.

I was beginning to think I was some kind of asshole-attractor.

Molly, the receptionist out front knocked on my door as she walked in. "She's out front. She wants to see you."

Her voice was sympathetic and partly weary.

I groaned. I knew exactly who "she" was. Mrs. Luster was the epitome of a thorn in my side. She had been coming here since I started working behind this desk several years ago. I dreaded the times she or her children had to make a visit to the office. It always resulted in about a pound of paperwork for me. She was insistent that her insurance company pay every last dime of every single one of her bills. If they didn't approve the whole visit or treatment, she would have me recode it and send the invoice out again. If that didn't work, she would have me bill her secondary insurance. Yes, she had secondary insurance. It was a good thing to have. But frankly, this woman abused the system and she used me to do it.

And if I even looked like I was going to tell her she owed a portion of her bill, fireworks ensued.

There were days I considered calling in sick when I thought I had to deal with her.

"Can this day get any better?" I muttered.

"I could tell her to make an appointment..." Molly offered.

"She doesn't have one?"

She shook her head. "No, she said this concerns a bill from a previous appointment."

I groaned. I knew the bill. I'd resubmitted it like three times already. I managed to get the portion she owed down to about fifty dollars. I thought—no, I'd hoped she would just pay it and be quiet.

I guess my naivety extended to more parts of my life beyond men.

"Just send her in. Might as well get it over with."

Molly seemed relieved. I didn't blame her. She was brave to offer to make Mrs. Luster schedule an appointment because the woman would likely cause a scene. "Thank you," she mouthed and then went to fetch the dragon—I mean, woman.

I pulled up her account, which I actually knew by heart, and then waited for her to enter. It didn't take long.

She breezed into the room, all five feet of her. For a woman so small, she sure commanded a lot of space and attention. In her hands she clutched the bill. In the depths of her brown eyes churned the will of a WWE fighter.

The weight I felt on my shoulders earlier seemed to intensify. I cleared my throat and sat up a little straighter, battling against the heaviness I was feeling.

"I got another bill today. *This* one threatened to send me to the collection agency if it's not paid by next month."

"Mrs. Luster, I've submitted that particular bill three times. The point of the matter is your son broke his arm. It was an unfortunate accident. This office was very happy to help him heal and look after his care. How is your son, by the way?"

"Chandler is just fine." She sniffed.

"That's wonderful news," I said cheerfully while my inner self was barfing. "I hope you will understand sometimes the insurance just won't cover bills entirely, no matter how many times I resubmit them."

"Change the coding."

This woman should have been a lawyer.

"I have. Many times. There are no codes left that apply to this charge."

"Are you saying you refuse to do your job?" she shrieked.

Tryst

The headache behind my eyes intensified. "Mrs. Luster..." I began, not really sure what I would say to get through to this nutcase, but knowing I had to do something.

"I guess I shouldn't be surprised," she muttered. "You're nothing but an incompetent bimbo."

I gasped. "Excuse me?"

She looked pointedly at my chest, which was extremely offensive. "Well, it's clear your skills are not why you're kept around."

Like a brittle piece of plastic left out in the cold too long, I snapped. I rose out of my chair to my full height, which happened to be two whole inches taller than her. "That was extremely uncalled for. There is no reason to be rude. I am very good at what I do—"

"If you were, you would fix this!" she demanded, shoving the bill between us.

"Just pay it!" I burst out.

Dr. Asik pushed my door open all the way and stepped inside. He was dressed in black slacks, a dress shirt, and a white doctor's coat. "Ladies?" He began, looking between us. "Is there a problem?"

"This woman is an incompetent excuse for a billing representative," Mrs. Luster responded immediately.

I felt my face redden under her attack. I really didn't have the patience for this today. "Dr. Asik, this patient is having a problem with paying her bill. She's become upset and insulting."

I thought the woman was going to explode. Her eyes narrowed and her chest puffed out with the huge breath she drew in. "Let me tell you something," she spat. "I have been coming to this office with my family for many years now. It's become quite the chore to deal with your billing manager." She looked directly at the doctor. "I'm thinking perhaps I should take my business elsewhere."

"Please, God," I prayed. Yeah, I said it out loud. It wasn't my most professional moment, but it was certainly nicer than I wanted to be.

Dr. Asik flicked a gaze at me and then turned his blue eyes and charming smile on Mrs. Luster. "I certainly hope you don't take your family elsewhere, ma'am," he said smoothly and in a calm voice. For a guy with such a giant ego, he had good bedside manner. Even if I knew it was fake. "You are a valued part of the practice family. How is your son, by the way?"

Oh, geez. What was this, ass kisser anonymous?

"He's doing well, thank you. He's a popular boy, has the cast filled with signatures."

Dr. Asik chuckled warmly. "I just bet he does." He glanced down at the bill being crushed in her hand. "Why don't you let me take care of that?" he said, reaching for the bill.

The bottom dropped out of my stomach. Seriously? He was going to reward her for bad behavior? What a douchebag.

"I would appreciate that." She sniffed and gave me a victorious look.

I thought about throwing my cup of pens. At. Her. Face.

After she surrendered the bill to the doctor, he looked at me. "We should talk."

My mouth ran dry and my heart rate accelerated. Really? This crazy comes in here and throws a fit because I was doing my job, and *I* get in trouble?

Could this day get any worse?

I cleared my throat. "Of course."

Before leaving, Mrs. Luster glanced at me and I thought I might have seen a flash of regret in her eyes before it was gone and she exited the room with her haughty stance and posture.

The door snapped with finality when the doctor closed it behind her. I sank down into my chair wearily.

"That was poorly handled," he said.

My eyes shot up. "That woman is a complete monster. Every time she comes in here, we all cringe."

"I see," he said, mulling over my words.

I remained silent. The words that wanted to make their way out of my mouth were not very nice.

"You've worked here a long time," he said, sticking the bill in the pocket of his coat. "You're not a team player."

"A team player?" I echoed.

"That's right. All the other girls might cringe when difficult patients walk in, but unlike you, they handle those people with grace."

"That woman—" I began, feeling the intense urge to take up for myself.

He held up his hand to stop me. "I have kept you on because you are very good at coding and with the numbers. But working with others, being part of a team, is not your strong suit."

"I didn't realize I was on a team. I'm the only billing rep you have here."

He sighed and stepped closer to the edge of my desk. I swear he was getting off on towering over me. An intense urge to stand burned through me. I ignored it. I really didn't want him to think I was challenging him.

"That's the problem, Talie. The people in this office are a team. We go out for drinks occasionally. We stay late to get to know each other, and the other women here are always ready and willing to let me know they enjoy their job."

And I no longer had suspicions that the girls here were sleeping with him. Now I *knew* they were.

"Maybe if you were more of a team *player*," he said, emphasizing the word player, "I might be able to overlook the aversion to working with others and being hostile toward the patients."

"Hostile!" I demanded. That was just dramatic. My chair slid backward up against the wall when I stood.

He looked me over. His lingering eyes made me feel slimy. "Is everything all right?" he asked. "You're looking a little frayed."

"I'm fine," I replied curtly.

"Maybe you would like to have a drink after hours and tell me what caused you to be less than courteous toward this patient today?"

Silence fell between us. It was like a heavy snowfall over the room, muffling all sounds. I was a smart girl. I could read between the lines. And what he was really saying was, *Sleep with me like everyone else here and I will overlook what happened today.*

Why was it I couldn't get my own husband to sleep with me, yet this clump nugget was more than willing?

He looked at me encouragingly, nodding yes like that was going to somehow hypnotize me into repeating the answer.

I smiled sweetly. "Thank you for your concern, Dr. Asik. I'm afraid I'm busy tonight. And every night after that."

His eyes turned dark. His lips pinched. "Are you sure?"

Once again, I was misjudged by a man who thought I would literally give in to what he wanted. "One hundred percent."

He sighed like there was a pain in his side. "I'm afraid I'm going to have to let you go."

Shock rippled through me. "What?"

"As I said, you're not a team player and you demonstrated today that putting the patient first was difficult for you. Here at this office we strive to make the patient feel as comfortable as possible. Gather your things. You're fired."

He left the office without another glance.

I sank down in the desk chair that was no longer mine.

I guess that answered that.

This day most certainly could get worse.

4

Talie

We met at an outdoor restaurant, one of the
nicest in Raleigh. Over the smooth concrete patio was
a huge white gazebo dripping in spring flowers in the
color of lilac. The tables were all pristine white and
the white chairs were adorned with apple-green and
strawberry-colored cushions. It wasn't hot, partially
because it was only eleven a.m. but also because there
were ultra-quiet, discreet fans tucked around the
eatery to ensure a cooling breeze.

The servers were all dressed in white with the
men wearing bright-green ties and the females
wearing strawberry-colored ones. All of them walked
with grace and many carried large glass pitchers of
lemonade and ice water.

My steps faltered when I saw Jack sitting at the
table with Joanna. I rarely saw him, except for
holidays and special occasions. In fact, I didn't think
I'd ever seen him this early in the day on a workday.

As I made my way to the table, I couldn't help
but notice what a beautiful couple they made. Joanna

with her thick, luxurious hair that was always sleek, even sitting outside in the southern humidity. She was wearing a lemon-yellow cardigan with a necklace made of white metal flowers. Her figure was thin and tight despite giving birth to twins. Jack was sitting to her left and he was dressed in a dove-gray suit, white dress shirt, and peacock-blue silk tie. His face was shaven and smooth, and his hair was the color of caramel. In all honesty, I'd always thought he looked a little like a young version of the late John F. Kennedy.

Neither of them spoke. In fact, they looked off in opposite directions, and it struck me that while they looked beautiful together, they didn't look like they were connected at all. Of course, I knew better. Joanna's life was perfect, right down to her marriage. I knew she and Jack were close. She just thought showing too much affection in public was inappropriate.

They looked up when I approached the table. Joanna smiled and Jack stood up like the southern gentleman he was. After I was seated across from him, he settled beside my sister again.

"Thank you for meeting me for lunch," I said.

"Of course," Joanna said, looking me over. I felt the scrutiny of her gaze, but for once I didn't worry about it. I was too tired to care that I likely didn't measure up. "You look tired."

Being cheated on, fired from my job, and sleeping on my best friend's couch (because I was practically homeless) made a girl sort of tired. After getting canned at work yesterday, I went back to Claire's and had a good cry. Then I cleaned her apartment (I thought maybe cleaning could be my new therapist since I had to fire Dunkin Donuts) before drowning my sorrows in a couple margaritas.

My life was literally falling apart and I had no idea where to even begin to rebuild it. It was almost too much too soon. I walked around feeling the weight of a thousand pounds. It was hard to breathe, hard to move, and the constant nagging of my worried thoughts threatened to drive me slowly insane.

This was not how my life was supposed to be.

I decided not to comment on the fact I looked tired. Instead, I changed the subject. "I'm surprised to see you here," I said to Jack.

He smiled and sipped at his ice water. "You're family," he said simply.

The simple statement eased a little of that pressure in my chest. I might be losing everything, but I did still have my family. I took a moment before I replied, afraid my wobbly voice would betray me.

"Joanna asked you to draw up divorce papers?"

She made a little sound of protest, but I ignored her. The waitress approached our table and Joanna waved her away, requesting a few more moments.

"I have to say, I was surprised by the request," Jack said.

"Well, I was surprised when I found Blake having sex with another woman," I snapped.

"Talie!" Joanna scolded. She looked around to make sure no one had heard. Like I was admitting to some contagious disease.

"What do you want me to say, Jo-Jo?" I asked wearily. "I can put a bow on it and make it sound prettier, but it's still the same."

"This is what I was afraid of," she said, glancing at Jack. Their eyes met and they did that silent husband-wife communication thing.

Blake and I never did that.

"I'm sitting right here," I reminded them.

Joanna sat back and Jack leaned forward. "Are you sure you've thought this through?" he asked. "You're under duress. You aren't yourself. Maybe you should take some time and think."

And that was why Jack was here. Joanna wanted backup. She thought he might talk me out of a divorce.

I looked him straight in the eye. "Have you ever cheated on my sister?"

Joanna gasped and sat forward. Jack seemed unperturbed by the question. Damn lawyers always kept their cool.

"Of course I haven't."

"And if you did, would you expect Joanna to stay with you?"

He cleared his throat, finally showing a little bit of unease.

"This is absurd, Natalie," she hissed, using my full name.

"Would you?" I asked her. "Stay with him?"

"We have children," she said, as if that explained everything.

I took that as a yes.

I lost a little respect for my sister in that moment. Maybe it wasn't fair of me to judge her, but wasn't that what she was doing to me at this very moment?

"Can I see the papers?" I turned to Jack.

He reached below the table and pulled a black briefcase into his lap. The stack of papers was neat and tidy, all stapled together with a single staple. A stack of papers and a pen was all I needed to end my marriage. To change my life. It seemed that after I promised to love someone forever through the good and bad, it shouldn't be so easy to undo all those promises.

"Read through them. If you have any questions, just call me," Jack said gently.

"Do you have a pen?" I asked.

"Talie," Joanna said. "You will not sign those here. Please think about this. Signing them would be a mistake."

"You really think so?" I asked, sitting back while the waitress returned to fill all our glasses with icy water. Jack ordered an appetizer for the table, and she left us alone once more.

"Talie," Joanna said empathically. How is it that my older sister could always put the kind of emotion into her voice that only a sister could? It's like my heart just automatically responded to that tone. Like it was a golden retriever trained to her command.

"Blake is a good man. His father built a very successful construction company that has become the number one go-to builder in Raleigh. Blake is poised to take over that company. He is very smart and business savvy. He's going places, places you will go if you stay together."

What kind of places was she talking about? Because the only place I could think about when I thought about staying with Blake was hell.

"I thought you wanted a home and a family?" she asked.

"I do." It was what I wanted more than anything. I guess I was old-fashioned that way. It wasn't the way a modern woman should be thinking. I certainly was all for women's equality, but there was something wonderful (to me) about having children and watching them grow, about having a home that I loved where I could water my roses and bake cookies in the kitchen. Was it really so wrong to just want a husband to love me, to think I'm beautiful, and to be surrounded by my children and grandchildren?

I thought I was going to have all that with Blake.

"You can still have that."

"He cheated on me," I said, my voice hollow and raw.

"It was a mistake. Surely by now he's seen the error of his ways. He knows what it's like to come home to a house without you in it. Have you even talked to him?"

I shook my head.

She sighed. "At least talk to him. See what he has to say. Maybe he wants to make amends."

She sounded so reasonable. Like it was all so possible. She made me feel like perhaps I overreacted. I glanced at Jack.

He nodded.

"I'll talk to him," I said. Joanna smiled. "But after that, I'm giving him the separation papers." I didn't bother to look at her reaction. Instead, I looked at Jack. "How long until the divorce can be finalized?"

"In North Carolina, you have to be separated for one year before the divorce can go through."

My lungs deflated. "An entire year?"

He nodded.

I guess a divorce wasn't as simple as paper and pen after all. I didn't know if I could deal with this for an entire year. That seemed so long. I needed to get those separation papers signed as soon as possible so that one year could start.

The waitress came back with a large dish of some kind of dip and a basket of bread and set it between us on the table. My stomach lurched. I picked up the papers and tucked them under my arm. "I just remembered I can't stay."

I stood up, muttering an apology. "You two have a wonderful lunch." Joanna looked like she was ready to try and change my mind. I'd had enough of that already. "Thanks Jack," I said and then raced away, turning the corner of the building and stopping to breathe a sigh of relief.

I pulled out my cell phone and hit a few buttons.

He answered on the first ring. His voice was like a sharp spear directly into my heart. I took a deep breath, ignoring the pain.

"We need to talk."

5

Talie

We met at the scene of the crime, aka: the house we shared up until two days ago. I knocked on the door when I arrived, the action totally strange and awkward. Who knocks on their own door?

But it wasn't my door anymore.

I needed to remember that. This apartment ceased to be my home the moment I walked out rolling a few large suitcases behind me.

I would do what Joanna asked. I would talk to Blake, see where his head was. After this conversation, maybe I would understand what happened. Maybe, just maybe, I would learn he really was regretful. For a fleeting moment, I imagined a grief-stricken Blake begging me to forgive him so we could start over again.

I wouldn't have to leave my life. I wouldn't have to abandon my dream of a family and a home. I wouldn't have an entire year of separation to endure. Just the thought of everything going back to normal again eased a little of the tension that coiled at the base of my neck.

And then he opened the door.

Blake was a good-looking man and he exuded charm. It practically dripped from his pores. I used to joke and tell him he didn't need cologne because his natural pheromones made women fall at his feet.

I didn't really think that joke was funny anymore.

He had a head of thick, dark hair he wore slightly long and pushed back in waves off his face. His skin was olive-toned and his eyes were dark. He looked like the Italian he was. His lips were full and lush, he had dimples on his cheeks when he smiled, and his teeth were white and straight.

A few of my co-workers (well, EX-co-workers now) called him Gaston because he looked just like the guy in *Beauty and the Beast* who thought Belle should marry him. I never before saw the resemblance. But I did today.

And having seen *Beauty and the Beast* several times, I realized calling him Gaston wasn't really a compliment. Sure he was a looker, but he was also a complete ass.

"Talie," he said warmly. The sound of my name on his lips once threatened to send me into a puddle of mush. He opened the door all the way. "You know you don't have to knock."

"I think I do," I said, brushing past him and into the apartment.

The tan leather couches, wooden coffee table, and various neutral throw pillows tossed on the furniture were exactly the same. The landscapes on the walls, the oversized clock my parents bought us for Christmas, the way the dining room table leaned just a bit because one of the legs was mysteriously a little too short... it was all the same.

So why did it feel so different?

I stood in the center of the room, clutching the envelope of papers, taking it all in and trying not to feel torn and devastated. The words ripped from my throat before I could even think.

"How could you?"

I turned, my blurry eyes focusing on the man I honestly thought I would spend forever with. He swallowed, the thick Adam's apple in his throat bobbed, and I stared at the open V the collar of his white dress shirt made against his skin.

"I'm sorry you had to see that."

But he wasn't sorry for doing it? a voice demanded in the back of my mind.

"Would you be sorry if you hadn't got caught?" I asked, wandering farther into the apartment. "Would you still be sleeping with her while I wondered why our sex life dropped off the face of this earth?"

He blanched. "You know I've been under a lot of stress at work." He began. "Dad has been really putting the pressure on me to step up to the helm."

I held up my hand. "Yes, I know your work schedule is very demanding. Yet you still found time to fit in some quality time with your secretary. Why? Why not me?"

"It's over," he said.

"You fired her?" I asked, shock rippling through me. Maybe he really was sorry.

"You know I can't do that!" he said. "She'd sue the company for sexual harassment. Do you know what something like that could do to the company's reputation?"

How convenient. He was forced to keep her on. Forced to continue working with her. "It must be horrible to worry about what people will say when they learn what a cheating scumbag you are."

A muscle ticked in the side of his jaw. "Natalie," he warned.

"I had Jack draw up separation papers." I pulled the stack of documents out of the envelope and then fished a pen out of my purse. "It's marked where we need to sign."

"You can't be serious." He actually sounded surprised.

I raised an eyebrow. "What did you think would happen?"

"This is just extreme!" he said, flinging his hands up in the air. "I didn't say anything when you packed your bags and left. I didn't say anything when you moved into Claire's apartment. I didn't even give you a hard time when you refused to answer any of my phone calls."

"What the hell do you want? A medal?" My insides began to boil. He acted like I was the one being unreasonable. Did I know him at all?

"But I'm drawing the line at separation papers, Talie," he said, like he was the lord of all.

"You can draw as many lines as you want." I sniffed. "After you sign these papers. I'll even loan you my pen."

He made an angry growl in the back of his throat. "I am not signing those papers."

"Do you really want to make this harder than it needs to be?"

"Do you?" He crossed his arms over his chest.

"Me?" I choked. "*You* are the one who cheated. *You* are the one with no regard for my feelings. *You* are responsible for this, *not* me."

"So I had a little fling. A tryst. It meant nothing to me."

"It's not nothing to me!" I shouted.

"The neighbors…" He reminded me.

I rolled my eyes. "That's all you care about, isn't it? Appearances. You care more about how a divorce will look than actually losing me."

"That's not true."

"It isn't?"

He sighed like I was being a petulant child.

"Then why haven't you apologized for what you did. Why haven't you told me that you love me and only me? Why haven't you begged me for forgiveness?"

"I tried calling you."

"You knew where I was. Did you come by? Did you make an attempt to seek me out?" I pressed, emotion and anger welling up inside me until I felt overfull and about to burst. "You didn't because you don't care enough."

"I was giving you time to cool off. To see reason."

"And what 'reason' is that?"

"We are not getting a separation."

"You're right. I want a divorce."

The words fell between us like an iron anvil. I couldn't help but notice the shock deep in his eyes. Was my reaction really that surprising?

"You can't divorce me," he said haughtily. He might have well said, *Don't you know who I am?*

I didn't bother to reply. Instead, I went over to the dining room table where I laid the papers out and proceeded to sign all the places marked with a yellow arrow. When I was finished, I looked up.

"Talie," he said, coming forward. He took the pen out of my hand and laid it on the table. He took me by the shoulders and turned me to face him. "I'm sorry that I hurt you."

"You did," I admitted, my voice low.

"I know, baby," he said, drawing me into his chest and wrapping his arms around me. "We can get through this. We can put it behind us and move on. Don't you want to have a baby?"

He knew I wanted a baby. I wanted one passionately.

"Everything's changed," I said, my voice muffled against him.

He made a sound of disagreement and stroked the back of my head. I suddenly felt like I was a dog being patted on the head. "Nothing's changed if you don't want it to be. Tear up these papers. Come home. I'll take over the company and we can start a family. You'll be a mother just like you always dreamed."

Blake palmed my face and pulled me back to look into my eyes. I couldn't stop the tears from welling up inside them. He was offering me everything we planned. Everything I wanted.

"What about *her*?" I said bitterly.

"Don't think about her," he said gently. "*You're* my wife. You're the one I chose to marry. The one I chose to give my name."

He made it sound like I won the lottery or something. What about love?

"Once the baby comes, you'll be so busy you won't even have time to think of her. I'll be discreet and—"

I jerked like he slapped me. He might as well have the way his words stung. "You'll be discreet?" I said, yanking myself away.

He sighed wearily.

"You mean to tell me you have no intention of not sleeping around on me?"

I always thought of Blake as a smart man... but I'd never heard anything more asinine come out of anyone's mouth. Ever.

"I'm a successful, powerful man," he replied. "I have needs that you just can't fulfill."

Oh. My. God.

Did he really just say that? Out loud? To my face?

I was speechless. Completely and utterly speechless.

He must have taken my silence for compliance because the idiot shoved his foot even farther down his throat. "But, baby, you are my only wife. The mother to my unborn children. It will be you at my side for all my achievements, your name splashed across the business pages in connection to mine. You'll never want for anything."

"Except a husband who loves me. Who respects me. Who wants only me."

"This isn't some fairytale, Talie. This is the real world."

I didn't realize love and respect was only for the movies. Silly me.

I picked up the pen. "Sign the papers."

His eyes widened.

"If you think I'm the type of girl who will sit home and take care of your kids while you go shove your dick into any hole that will take you, just so I can have the prestige of your name, then you have no clue who the hell you married."

Twin spots of pink flushed his cheeks. "That was crude."

"Yeah? Well, it's nothing compared to what I'm thinking."

"We're married. For better or worse. We are not getting divorced."

"Oh, we are," I said, rising up to my full five feet two inches. "And if you don't sign these papers right now, the name that you so graciously gave me on our wedding day will be filling up the gossip columns around here. Whatever will your daddy say about that?"

He paled. "You wouldn't."

"Freaking try me."

He studied me for long moments, and I didn't back down. I meant it. I was so utterly shocked and horrified by the things he just said to me that I could barely breathe. But I wasn't going to let him see that. He'd only try to use it to his advantage. I was going to be a freaking pillar of strength until I left here.

He must have realized because he signed the papers.

"This isn't over," he said, handing me back the pen.

"Oh, but it is."

He pursed his lips. "I changed all the passwords on the bank accounts. Don't think of trying to clean me out again."

"Oh…" I made a little shocked face. "I thought that was *our* money and not just yours."

"You know damn well who brings home the bacon," he snapped. "Your job is basically something to fill your time."

I didn't bother mentioning I was no longer employed.

That would be embarrassing.

Thank goodness I "cleaned him out" when I did. At least now I had enough money to last me a few months before I would be totally broke. By then, I would hopefully have another job.

I picked up the papers, the papers making our separation official. "I'll have these filed immediately."

"Enjoy your little tantrum now, Talie," Blake called behind me. "Because when you come back to me, I will not tolerate this kind of behavior."

I laughed.

"Laugh now," he replied. "You won't be laughing when you realize I'm the only man that will ever want you."

His words pierced something inside me. Something close to my heart withered a little. Those words hurt me, probably more than they should. I knew the reason they hurt so much was because he was voicing a fear I never wanted to admit.

The truth was no one had been interested before Blake, and I secretly realized no one else would be after him either.

Even so, I kept walking.

I'd rather be single than married and utterly alone.

6

Talie

I drove straight to Jack's office and gave the papers to his assistant. I made her promise to get them filed that day. After vowing she would do it, I left before someone could tell Jack I was there. I wasn't up for another "family intervention" about my marriage.

I kept my end of the deal. I talked to Blake. It was offensive and frankly disturbing. How could I have been so wrong about him? Sure, he'd always had an ego, and yes, he knew he was successful. But I truly had no idea he had such a… a… good ol' fashioned southern boy hidden beneath his exterior.

You think you know a guy…

Maybe I had seen the signs of the real him. Maybe I just didn't want to admit what kind of guy he really was, because if I did, I would also have to admit I let myself get duped. That I was just as guilty for his behavior because I gave him the impression I would be okay with it.

It was a mistake. A mistake I was correcting.

Since it was too early in the day to start drinking (hey, a girl has to have her standards), I pointed my stuttering car toward the store Claire managed. I couldn't really afford to shop right now since I was unemployed, but I could look… and maybe buy myself *one* thing. After the last few days, I think I earned something sparkly and new.

Her "office" was on the corner of a popular street in Raleigh. Just about everyone I knew shopped there. They had the best clothes by the best designers and their accessories were always flying off the shelves.

It was a mainstream store, with many locations across the US, so the prices weren't completely ridiculous like some of the specialty boutiques in this area.

The interior was brightly lit and well air-conditioned. Even though it was early in the day, shoppers milled around, most of them with purchases already draped in their arms. I browsed around for a bit, decompressing from the morning. Even though I was shopping, I barely paid attention to the things I was looking at because my thoughts were still focused on the things Blake said to me.

He thought I would allow him to sleep around. He expected me to be grateful that he chose me to be his wife. He made me sick. And I won't lie; his words were a huge blow to my self-esteem. I never thought I was the prettiest or the smartest, but I never really thought I was unworthy of anyone's full love either.

But that's exactly what he implied. He implied I wasn't enough to keep him happy. He implied *I wasn't enough.*

"Talie?" a familiar voice said from behind. I spun, blinking away the silent accusation.

"Hey, Claire," I said, mustering a smile for my best friend. She looked good in a cobalt-blue lace blouse, a pair of white skinny jeans, and her sassy red hair all styled out in an arranged tousled mess.

She was enough to keep a man happy.

"What happened?" she asked, her eyes narrowing on my face.

"I signed the separation papers."

She grabbed me by the wrist and led me through the store toward the back where we went through a door with a sign that read: "Employees Only." After making a sharp right into a small office, she closed the door and dropped down behind her desk with a sigh. "I hate inventory."

"Inventory sucks." I agreed just because that's what BFFs did. They agreed with each other. I'd never actually done inventory before so I wouldn't know, but I would take her word for it. That thought gave me an idea. "Is this place hiring?"

She gave me a wary look. "Actually we are. For sales associates."

"You don't think I would make a good employee?"

"Of course you would. I just can't imagine subjecting you to inventory."

I laughed. "Well, getting a paycheck might be nice."

"You're trained in billing and coding for doctors and hospitals."

"Numbers," I replied. "Isn't that what inventory is? Counting?"

"Touché."

"Can I have an application?"

"You can have the job if you want it," she said, waving away my request like it was a pesky technicality.

"Don't you want my references?" I lifted a brow.

"Nah." She grinned. "I know where you live."

I laughed.

"You didn't come here for a job. And you didn't come here to buy that god-awful purse you're carrying around."

I glanced down at the purse. I hadn't even realized I was still clutching it. It *was* ugly. I set it on her desk with a look of disdain.

"We got in a shipment of Michael Kors bags this morning. To die for. You should go through the stash before we put them on display."

"Where are they?" I asked, perking up. Maybe a new bag would make me feel better. It certainly would make me look better.

I had a slight obsession with purses.

Blake said I had too many.

It was exactly why I needed another one.

"So you saw him," she said, steering the conversation back to the reason I was here.

"Yes."

"How was it?"

"He apologized that I caught him in bed with his secretary. And then he told me he wanted to have a baby."

"He played the family card," she said. Claire knew how much I wanted a family and kids. Up until this point, Blake hadn't wanted to start a family yet. He was too focused on his career. "Maybe he really is sorry."

"Then he went on to say he would be discreet in his future affairs and I wouldn't notice because I'd be too busy being a mother."

"Tell me you're kidding."

"I'm not kidding."

"And that explains that ugly-ass bag you were carrying around." She sighed.

I grimaced and looked at the bag. It was the color of puke. And it smelled weird.

"Do I have the words COMPLETE IDIOT stamped across my forehead?"

"Of course not. He's just a complete ass."

"I made him sign the papers. I threatened his good family name." I glanced at Claire. "He said it wasn't over."

"And people wonder why I'm still single," she mused. After her comment, she glanced at me, guilty. "Sorry."

"Don't be. I wish I'd never gotten married."

We lapsed into silence.

"I'm homeless, about to get divorced, and out of a job."

"I just gave you a job." Claire pointed out.

I gave her a dark look.

"Oh, sorry. Was I interrupting your pity parade?"

"Yes."

She grinned. The phone on her desk rang. She rolled her eyes and reached for it. "Claire Fuller," she answered. "Mom!" she said a few seconds later. "I told you not to call me at work unless it was an emergency! ... The state of Aunt Ruth's bunions are not an emergency. And frankly, I don't want to hear about it at all." She made a motion and I smiled.

Claire's family was a kooky bunch, but I loved them anyway. "I can't talk right now. Talie is here."

She paused and I heard the low chattering of her mother on the end of the line.

"She's getting a divorce. Blake cheated on her. She's staying at my place."

I made a sound as she rattled off my business like it was old news. *Geez, just tell everyone, why don't you.*

Her mother's chattering got louder. Claire made a sound of agreement. Then she looked at me and made the talking signal with her hand as her mother kept yapping.

"That serious?" Claire said, interrupting. "For a bunion?" Her tone was doubtful. "How long?"

My eyes wandered toward the ugly purse. Maybe if I tied a beautiful scarf around the handle and pinned a sparkly broach on the side it wouldn't be so hideous. It just seemed wrong to leave that poor bag so unsightly.

Claire snapped her fingers at me as if she could read my thoughts. When I looked up, she shook her finger at me like I was a dog who went pee on the floor.

"Mom!" She interrupted. "Who's taking care of Ruth's house?"

"I'll just go shop," I mouthed, getting up to escape her office.

Claire gave me the eyes of death.

Eyes of death = promise of great torture later if I moved from my chair.

"What about Salty?" she asked.

I walked to the door, defying her death stare. What was she going to do that hadn't already been done to me in the past couple days?

"Talie will do it!" she said.

I stopped and turned, wondering what in the hell she was saying. "Do what?" I said.

"Mom," she said. "Mom!" she screeched. "I get it. I'll be over after work." She slammed the receiver down and made a sound of relief. "That woman could talk fifty-year-old wallpaper off a wall. It'd peel itself off just to get away!"

"What the hell did you just drag me into?"

"Aunt Ruth had bunion surgery. Apparently, bunions are very painful." She shrugged. "Anyway, my dad drove down to Topsail to get her. She's staying with them while she heals. I guess she has to stay off her foot for a while, and since she lives alone, Mom wanted her here."

"Well, I hope she's okay."

"It's a bunion," she said dryly.

I suppressed a giggle.

"Anyway, Aunt Ruth's house is going to be sitting empty. So I volunteered you to housesit."

"You what!"

"It's great timing. Your calendar is wide open and you need a vacation."

"I need to put my life back together."

"So what are your plans? You honestly want to work here, as a sales girl, and sleep on my couch forever?"

Of course I didn't. It's just... this was all so sudden I had no idea what to do. I didn't have a backup plan.

"Exactly." Claire surmised by the look on my face. "Aunt Ruth lives on the beach. Like, literally the sand is at her backdoor. Go stay there, smell the ocean air, take long walks on the beach… get the hell out of town. You need it."

It certainly wasn't the worst idea I'd ever heard. At least if I wasn't here, I wouldn't have to listen to Joanna tell me what a huge mistake I was making.

"I guess I could go for a few days."

"At least a week, Talie," Claire said.

"Fine."

She grinned. "There's a whole rack of new bathing suits out there. You can pick one out with the new purse."

"Yeah, because this week hasn't been shitty enough. Now I have to subject myself to bathing suit shopping."

Her phone rang again. She groaned.

"I'll just go look around."

She nodded. Just as she picked up the phone, I remembered something. "Claire?" I asked.

She held the phone away from her as she looked at me.

"Who's Salty?"

"My aunt's cat."

As I wandered out into the store, steering clear of the bathing suits (evil things), I had to laugh. I laughed so loud a nearby woman gave me a strange look.

My life was reduced to living with a cat. I was turning into a cat lady.

Of course, at this point, I'd take a cat over a man any day. Men weren't to be trusted, especially with matters of the heart. Hell, maybe when I got home from vacation, I would get a cat of my own.

I laughed again, this time a little more to myself. I had to laugh. If I didn't, I might start crying and never stop.

7

Talie

Topsail Island was located on the coast of North Carolina and was just over a two-hour drive from Raleigh. The island itself was approximately twenty-six miles long and completely surrounded by water. There were only two ways on and off the island and both of those ways were by bridge.

This wasn't the first time I'd ever been to Topsail. I'd come here many times as a kid with my parents and brother, but that seemed like a lifetime ago. This would be the first time I'd ever come here alone.

Coming alone wasn't depressing to me. If anything, it was refreshing. The more miles that slipped between Raleigh and me, the more at ease I felt. I did need this. I needed time to think, to process, and to feel. I didn't tell anyone where I was going; the only person that knew was Claire, and I made her promise not to tell a soul.

When I turned onto the two-lane road that would carry me to the island, I rolled the window down and let the thick, humid air swirl inside the car. The heady scent of salt pressed against my skin and lips. I knew if I were to stick out my tongue, the sharp taste would already be on my lips.

My hair blew around in the breeze, and for once I didn't worry about how tangled it was getting. It didn't matter. No one here knew me. No one here cared what I looked like. It was freeing to not have to worry who I might see at the grocery store or worry what someone might think.

The road was empty at this late hour. It was already after nine and the sky was dark. It always seemed darker at the beach. Without the lights of busy streets and strips of shopping centers, the sky took on a velvet quality that I didn't often get to see.

The shape of the bridge came into view, and I smiled. I couldn't wait to bury my toes in the sand. I looked ahead at the way the bridge rose up off the ground, supported on thick legs to curve up over the sound, the intercoastal waterway. Part of me was sad it wasn't light out because the views from the top of the bridge would be spectacular and go on for miles.

But there was always tomorrow.

Just as the road started to gradually lift and lead onto the bridge, my car made a very loud clunking sound and then groaned like it was going to come apart at any second.

Even though my foot was pressed on the gas, the car slowed considerably, idling along like a turtle who had nowhere it needed to be. "Come on!" I yelled at the dashboard as I gave the steering wheel a smack.

Suddenly, the wheel seemed extremely hard to steer. What usually was an easy, effortless task now seemed like something that required large muscles.

Did I mention I was lacking in the muscle department?

I applied the brakes and fought the Jetta to the side of the road. I wasn't about to try and make it over the bridge like this. My luck, I would plunge over the side and get eaten by a shark when I hit the water.

The loud rattling sounds the stupid car made drowned out the cadence of the ocean waves and caused some of the peace I found on my way here to disappear.

After several long moments of just sitting there, leaning my forehead on the steering wheel and asking God why I was cursed, I turned off the engine. The car stuttered and then died. I knew it wasn't going to turn back on.

"And the hits just keep on coming," I said out loud.

I opened the car door, leaving it open so the light would stay on for a few moments, and bent down to look for the hood release latch. After I found it and popped the hood, I stood there staring down in the dark at the insides of a car I couldn't see.

Then I remembered my phone. The flashlight app was handy in moments like this. Even with the engine and innards of the car visible, I had no clue what was wrong with it.

"I am so getting a new car." I sighed. I called up the number to AAA in my phone (I might not know how to fix cars, but I knew how to call people who did) and wondered how long it would take them to send a tow.

A pair of headlights appeared traveling in my direction. I raced around the side of the car and leapt into the driver's seat, slamming the door behind me.

After the way this week was going, I wouldn't be surprised at all if the person behind the wheel of that car was a serial killer out looking for his next victim.

The car slowed and pulled directly behind my car.

See? Total serial killer.

I heard the slam of the door and watched as a large, dark figure approached. I could make out nothing because his headlights turned him into nothing but a dark shadow.

The only thing I knew for sure was that it was a man. Unless, of course, it was a woman. Judging from the sheer size of the black shape, if it was, then she would have to be a professional body builder.

Seconds later, a darkened face appeared at my window.

"Car trouble?" he rumbled. His voice was deep and his southern accent was strong.

I screamed.

I forgot my window was down!

I jammed the key back into the ignition and turned over the engine. It made a puny, pathetic sound and stalled out. The windows were electric. I couldn't get it up if the car wouldn't start.

"Please don't kill me!" I burst out.

A laugh floated through the night air and wrapped around my body. He put one of his hands on the door so that it rested where the window should be, his fingers falling down the inside of the door.

I snatched the keys out of the ignition and swung down to stab the fleshy part of the back of his hand. Seconds before I made him bleed, he jerked away.

"I'm not going to murder you!" he shouted.

"Don't you yell at me!" I retorted.

"You tried to stab me!"

"You tried to kill me!"

"I stopped to see if you needed help. You know, because your junker car here stopped working."

"How dare you call it a junker?" I fumed. My car definitely was a junker, but I wasn't about to let him insult me. I'd had enough of men to last me a lifetime.

"Sweetheart, I call it like I see it," he drawled.

Damn if I didn't get goose bumps. His voice was like the velvet sky I was admiring only moments ago. "Well, okay, it's a piece of crap." I allowed. Obviously, his southern accent was making me stupid.

"I'm just going to take a look," he said. Before I could tell him no, he was walking around the front of my car. The glow of his headlights gave me a glimpse of the way his hips rotated when he walked.

He had long legs, the kind that owned the ground whenever he took a step. He was tall... at least six two. Other than that, I couldn't make out anything else about him. He was wearing a baseball hat and it was pulled down low, shading all of his face from the little light out here.

A light clicked on up front (he must have had the same app as me), and I saw him reaching down into the engine. The sound of something being pulled out of the car had me leaping out of my seat and rushing around the front.

"What the hell are you doing?" I demanded, horrified, as he pulled out this long, black thing. "Is that a snake?" I shrieked. Had I somehow run over that giant thing and it got caught in my engine?

He paused and looked up at me. "A snake?" he asked like he couldn't understand what I was saying. Then he shook his head. "It's the drive belt," he muttered, going back to pulling it out.

"Well, if it's supposed to be in there, why are you pulling it out?"

"This way when I go to kill you, I know you won't be able to get away."

I ran for my phone, which I left lying in the front seat. Forget AAA. I was calling the police!

His laugh stopped me in my tracks. "Are you always this gullible?"

"Only when people tell me they're gonna kill me," I snapped.

"The drive belt snapped. Half of it is shredded. The car isn't going to start until it's fixed."

"Oh," was all I could manage.

"And judging from what else I can see, I think there are some other issues in there too."

"Yeah, well, I'm not surprised."

"Where are you headed?" he asked, dropping the ruined belt on the ground.

"Topsail Island."

He made a sound that seemed to rumble out of his chest. "You have a house here?"

"I'm not telling you that!"

"You got someone you can call?" he asked, not seeming offended by my refusal to tell him a thing.

"Yeah." I turned away and dialed AAA and gave them my location. They said the tow truck could be forty-five minutes to an hour.

Wonderful.

Once I was done, I disconnected and threw the phone onto my front seat. "Thanks for stopping, but I have this under control."

"Just doing my gentlemanly duty," he said, tipping his hat. Beneath it was a mess of thick blond hair.

Something told me he was anything but a gentleman.

Without another word, he walked back to his car. That lazy, long-legged walk of his snagged my stare more times than I cared to admit.

After settling in my car, I leaned my head against the seat, thinking about calling Claire to tell her my latest disaster. After a few minutes, I realized I never heard the man drive away.

I glanced back and sure enough, his car was still sitting there. The interior of the car was too dark to make out if he was in there.

Pricks of fear lifted the hairs on my arms. Why was he still here? What was he doing back there in the dark?

Maybe he really was going to kill me after all.

8

Talie

Twenty minutes. That's how long I sat in my car, looking into the mirrors and wondering what the hell that man was doing.

Twenty minutes of torture was quite enough. So I positioned my keys between two fingers, with the pointy end sticking out, and called up 9-1-1 on my phone just in case I needed to place an emergency call for help. Even though it was summer, the air felt slightly chilly as I climbed out of the car. The breeze off the water made it feel cooler than it really was.

There was no point in tiptoeing. We were out in the wide open. He would see me coming. Besides, I wasn't trying to hide. I wanted to know what the hell he was doing. I walked closer to his car, gripping the key in my hand just a little bit tighter. As I drew closer, I saw a dark shape shift in the driver's seat.

He was sitting in his car. Why the hell was he sitting in his car?

The window rolled down with ease (his window actually worked) and his voice drifted toward me. "Need something?"

"Yeah, I need to know why you're sitting back here like a creepy stalker."

"Are you this suspicious of everybody?" he asked.

"Just of men who sit around on empty streets, watching women," I remarked. Maybe if I had been suspicious of the men in my past, I wouldn't be sitting here now.

He sighed and then from somewhere in the car, he produced what looked like a Blow Pop. I watched as he unwrapped the candy to reveal a red sucker, which I knew was filled with gum. He slid the candy between his parted lips and rolled it from one side of his mouth to the other. When it settled, the side of his cheek puffed out, creating a lump.

It was the first time I'd ever seen a grown man eat a sucker.

It seemed completely wrong the way he made something created for a child to appear sinful and inappropriate. I watched as he twirled the stick in his oversized hand and drew it out through his lips.

Something in my stomach hollowed out as I watched, and the center of my palms grew sticky.

"I'm not gonna hurt you," he said, his voice low.

I believed him.

'Course, we already established I wasn't the best judge of character.

"I'm just gonna sit here until the tow truck comes. You know…" He leaned out the window and tipped his head back a bit. I caught a better glimpse of his face.

Strong jaw. Unshaven. Angular cheekbones.

"Just to make sure no one tries to kill ya."

He grinned. His teeth glowed against the night. A little chuckle floated between us and then he stuck that red lollipop back into his mouth.

I squeezed my legs together. Suddenly, I felt really squirmy, like standing still was impossible.

"You're just going to sit there?"

"Yep."

Alrighty then. I walked back to my car but stopped halfway there and looked back. He hadn't moved.

I felt confident enough to place my cell in the front seat of my car. But rather than climbing in, I went around to the front, where the hood was still open. There was really no reason to leave it that way. I wasn't going to fix it. I would just let the mechanic do that. Hopefully I could get the tow guy to drop me at Aunt Ruth's place before carting my car off to wherever it was going to go.

I slammed the hood shut and stared down at the traitorous metal. If I didn't need it to drive back to Raleigh, I'd tell them to take it to the junkyard.

"Stupid car that stupid Blake insisted I keep for just one more year," I muttered. *"Just one more year and I'll buy you whatever you want."* What kind of man buys himself a brand-new car and let's his wife drive a bucket of bolts?

I spun away to stomp back to the driver's seat. But I didn't make it very far. My foot got tangled in the ruined drive belt coiled on the ground. I pitched forward, the stupid thing refusing to let me go. My arms shot out as I tried to balance, but it was no use.

I went tumbling over, tangling up in the black strap even more.

I let out a screech and hit the ground. The hard-packed dirt was jarring against my side. I rolled, trying to get up but couldn't. I pushed up onto my hands and feet (kind of like a downward dog position) and lifted one sandal-clad foot up and over. The belt pulled taut and sent me falling to the side. Unfortunately for me, I rolled down a hill.

I probably shouldn't have parked so close to the bridge and where it started to rise because the ground started to fall away.

I think I hit every pebble, every shell, and every stick on the way down the short little hill. "Ow!" I yelled as the stuff poked at me.

I skidded past a large bush of some kind, and I reached out, grasping it around the base with my hand. Finally, I stopped falling.

I lay there breathing rapidly, blinking the dirt and sand out of my eyes.

"This is what I get for trying to get away on vacation," I muttered as I yanked myself up into a sitting position. Not far off to the side was the water. If I'd kept going, I would have splashed right into the sound.

Squeezing pain cut into my thoughts as I became aware of a portion of the shredded belt wound around my ankle. It was being pulled and cutting into my skin. I rolled sideways, pulling the length out from under me and reaching down to untangle it from my skin.

Stinging from a few scrapes and cuts on my short-clad legs presented itself, and I sighed. I fought with the chord for long moments, unable to get it off.

I was about to yell in frustration when the dark shape of a man came over the hill and started toward me.

I knew it was the guy who wasn't going to kill me. I gave up on the belt tangled around me and watched as he stepped down the short hill with ease. He looked so graceful and self-assured, and here I was a lump that couldn't even close the hood of her car.

I was about to tell him I had the situation handled when he crouched down beside me. His closeness was unsettling. Not because I was afraid, but because I liked it. It was almost like a cloud had drifted and revealed the sun. The heat coming off his body was intoxicating. I hadn't even realized how cold I was until he showed me.

"Did you hurt yourself?" he asked.

"No, I'm just tangled up."

He shook his head and pulled out what looked like a Swiss Army knife from his jeans. The moonlight glinted off the blade when he flicked it open.

My hackles raised as my heart started to pound when he reached for me. I jerked away and he grunted. "I'm going to cut you lose. Don't move. You'll just get tangled more."

His fingers worked their way between my skin and the taut piece of chord wrapped around my ankle. I shivered and he paused. I felt his stare from beneath the brim of his hat, but I didn't dare look up. I couldn't. If I did, he might see I wasn't shivering because I was cold.

His skin was smooth. Smooth as satin. There wasn't a callous or rough spot on his hand. Even though he had to squeeze his touch beneath the belt, he was still gentle, like he honestly cared if he hurt me.

"Hold still," he said again, this time his voice a mere whisper. With a deft hand, he slid the blade under the chord and within seconds sliced through the bind. Once it was cut, he worked quickly to unwind the rest from my leg.

After he tossed it aside, his hands skimmed down my calf and my eyes closed. When was the last time someone touched me? Like really touched me?

I didn't know the answer.

And that realization made me incredibly sad. Emotion welled up in me and I fought against it. This wasn't the time to cry. This wasn't the time to decide I was some withering violet, because I most certainly was not.

"Are you cut?" he asked, smoothing his hands over the area that had been confined.

I cleared my throat. "I don't think so."

"Is it around you anywhere else?"

Was it wrong I wished it was? "No."

He removed his hands quickly, and I felt like a complete idiot for wishing they'd lingered. "Good," he said, standing. On his feet, he towered over me, making me feel vulnerable and weak. I didn't like to feel that way.

I started to stand and he reached for me, slipping his palm beneath my arm, and lifted, helping me to my feet. Even after I was standing, he kept hold of me, guiding my steps as I freed both my feet from the rest of the shredded belt.

"This is your fault, you know," I told him, kicking at the black stuff.

"My fault?" he choked.

"You're the one who piled this crap on the ground where I could trip and fall."

"Sweetheart, I've known you all of five minutes and even I know you would trip and fall over the wind. You certainly didn't need my help to go rolling down this hill."

I pulled my arm from his grasp, suddenly hating the way my body tingled beneath his touch. "Whatever," I retorted (yeah, it was the best I could come up with) and stomped up the hill.

When I got there, another pair of headlights was approaching and a large tow truck pulled up near my car.

Thank God.

I waved my arms just so he was sure he had the right car and then hurried around to the driver's side. A man wearing a pair of board shorts and a T-shirt stepped out. He didn't look at all how I expected him to look.

Yes, I was stereotyping.

But my idea of a tow truck driver wasn't some twenty-something man with a surfer outfit and sunglasses on his head (even at night).

"Car trouble?" he asked.

"Yes. I think it's the drive belt. But it could be more than that." I gestured to the Jetta.

"You have a place you want me to tow it?"

"I'm not from around here. I drove in from Raleigh."

"How long will you be here?"

"About a week."

He nodded. "Well, my dad owns a small garage in Surf City over on the island. He could have it fixed for ya before you leave."

"That would be wonderful," I said, thankful the car could be fixed so close by.

"Sweet," he said. "I'll just get ya towed up. Can I give you a ride somewhere?"

Suddenly, nerves got the best of me. Here I was accusing the last man who stopped to help me of trying to kill me, so how did I know this guy wasn't just pretending to be a tow truck driver? Maybe he didn't have a dad who owned a garage. Maybe he had a dad in county lockup, doing thirty to life for murder.

"Uhhh," I said, trying to stall as I thought it through.

"Rand, is that you?" the guy in the hat said, coming around the truck.

Rand laughed. "Yeah, dude. What the hell you doing here?"

"I saw her car and stopped to see if she needed help."

"Righteous."

You know you're at the beach when some "dude" says righteous.

"You working with your dad now?" he asked the kid, who seemed younger and younger as the minutes passed.

"Nah, just doing him a favor."

"Sweet. Well, I'll leave you to it. See you later."

Rand turned to ready the truck for towing and the man whose name I didn't know walked off without a backward glance.

"Wait!" I suddenly burst out, chasing after the man.

He stopped but didn't turn. I rushed over and stepped around him, tilting my head back to look up.

"You're just going to leave me with him?" I accused. "A stranger?"

"Suddenly you trust me?" he said. I swear there was a hint of amusement in his words.

"This isn't funny!" I whisper-yelled. "He could be dangerous!"

"Are you an actress?" he asked, knocking the bill of his hat back a little. I wished for a fleeting moment I could make out the color of his eyes.

"What?" I asked. "No."

"Well, you sure are a damn drama queen."

I made a disgusted sound. "I swear," I muttered as I turned away. "Men just like to insult women."

I only got about two steps when his hand shot out and grabbed my wrist. "What did you say?"

"Nothing." I tried to yank my arm away.

He tightened his grip. "Hey."

The softness in his tone caused me to go still. I glanced up.

"I've known Rand a long time. He's young, but he's a good kid. His dad's a good man."

"Okay."

He pulled on me just a little, enough to make me take a single step closer. Once again, I felt the heat off his body. It was utterly intoxicating.

"I wouldn't leave you here with him if I thought you were in danger." He spoke low.

The sound of his voice caused chills to race over my scalp. You know, the kind you get when you get a really good massage? Yeah, that kind. The good kind.

I nodded.

"I'd tell ya to stay out of trouble, but I really doubt that's going to happen."

I scowled as he released my wrist and walked away. Immediately, I covered the area with my other hand, trying to trap in the warmth he left behind, if only for a few moments. The skin around the area tingled... I liked it.

He drove away. He didn't look back. I was glad.

9

Talie

I was learning all kind of life lessons lately:

1. You don't always know someone like you think you do.

2. Getting fired from a job you hate still sucks.

3. Just because you tell your car not to break down doesn't mean it will listen.

4. Blake is a butthead.

And most recently:

5. I was not destined to become a cat lady.

Salty hated me. And not in the way of there was a stranger in the house and he needed to get used to it. In the way of *you better sleep with one eye open because he will claw you to death if you don't* kind of way.

From the minute I let myself into Aunt Ruth's beach house, he did nothing but hiss, yowl, and stare at me from within doorways with some kind of death ray glare.

I offered him cat treats, cheese, and even a can of tuna. He was having none of it. The one time he let me get close enough to put a treat under his nose, he took a swipe with his claws and made me bleed. I was left with one conclusion.

Salty = a furry demon.

Even though the cat may or may not have been the spawn of Satan himself, the view from the windows was more than worth the danger. The house was small, with two bedrooms and two bathrooms, the rest of the house being made up of an eat-in kitchen with a wooden table and a living room with tons of windows. Every room in the house had a view of the ocean (except for one of the bathrooms).

The windows spanned the length of the back of the house, offering panoramic views of the surf meeting the sand. Beyond the windows, the house sported a large, weathered wooden deck filled with lounge chairs for taking in the view. Stretching off the deck was a set of wooden stairs and a wooden path that led directly onto the sand. Between the house and the beach was a sand dune littered with seashells, tall grasses, and piles of sand.

Though small, the house was nice, with wicker furniture and soft linen cushions, light-painted walls, and a brightly patterned round ottoman as the coffee table. There was a small TV against the wall, sitting on a rustic-looking console table and photographs of the beach hanging on the walls. The kitchen was open to the living space and it offered white-painted cabinets, granite countertops the color of sand, and clean white appliances.

When Rand the tow truck driver dropped me off last night, I trudged into the house with my bags and dropped them by the front door. After standing on the deck outside, staring up at the starlit sky, I tried to make friends with Salty. That didn't go as planned, so I found the guest bedroom and collapsed on the bed.

The next thing I knew, the sun was rising up above the ocean and making the blue waves glimmer like diamonds in a glass case. The second I sat up in bed, I noticed the scowling from the bedroom door.

"What are you looking at?" I asked the white cat.

He swished his tail and sauntered away after giving me an angry hiss.

Still wearing the shorts and T-shirt I wore driving in last night, I padded out to the kitchen to get the demon cat some food. Maybe once he realized I was here to take care of him, he would get some manners.

I poured some kitty chow into his bowl and set it on the floor. Then I gave him fresh water and set it beside the food and called out to him. "Here kitty, kitty, kitty!"

Seconds later, he sauntered across the tile. "Your breakfast is served," I told him.

He reared back and swiped at me, scratching my leg. "Ow!" I yelled. "Bad kitty!"

He ignored me. I picked up my cell and punched in Claire's number.

"What?" she growled sleepily into the phone.

"Why aren't you up for work?"

"I'm off today."

"This cat is a demon. It hates me."

"Salty?" she asked.

"Please tell me there is only one cat in this house."

She yawned loudly. "Just one. Salty hates everyone but Aunt Ruth."

"And you didn't think that would be good to mention?"

"He's a little cat. How much trouble could he possibly be?"

"I'm bleeding, Claire," I said, deadpan.

"Get a Band-Aid." She yawned again.

"My car broke down on the side of the road last night."

"Oh my God! Are you okay?"

"I didn't wreck it," I said. "I had to have it towed."

"Ruth's car is there, isn't it? My dad drove her up here."

"Yeah, it's in the driveway."

"Keys should be in the kitchen. You can use her car when you need to," Claire replied.

"Thanks. I don't plan on going anywhere except out for groceries."

"Call me if the cat kills you."

"If it kills me, I won't be able to use the phone," I said, exasperated.

She laughed and then the line went dead.

The cat was still eating, and I made a wide arc around him, then went toward the windows and looked out at the gorgeous, sun-drenched view. Man, the beach was stunning. There was this instant feeling of peace that washed over me every time I looked out over the vast blue sea at the rolling waves and surf.

The sun had just risen, and the space where the sky met the water was a deep shade of blush. Not quite pink, but not quite peach either. It was one of those colors you only saw when a new day was dawning. It filled me with a sense of hope. A sense of renewal. Life as I knew it might be ending, but something else was being born.

I sighed and with the slight movement, I caught a glimpse of my reflection in the glass. Oh my word, I was frightening! No wonder the cat was so mean to me. I probably scared him silly walking around looking like this.

It was as if a flock of angry birds had turned my hair into a nest. When I said I didn't care what I looked like and how many tangles I got, I meant it, but this... this was just uncalled for. A girl had to have her standards.

I abandoned the view (regrettably) and went into the bathroom. My little duffle with all my shower supplies was sitting on the floor, and I rummaged through it to pull out my brush and detangling spray. I set it on the counter and looked in the mirror.

Oh, it was really bad.

The only thing that would fix the mess I had going on was a hot shower and half a bottle of conditioner. After I found a towel in the linen closet and pulled out the rest of my needed items, I climbed under the spray and got to work.

It felt good to wash away the travel. The stinging cuts on my legs from rolling down the hill smarted under the spray, and it reminded me of last night.

More specifically, the man who stopped to help me.

Even in the dark, I knew he was attractive. Too bad his good looks (well, what I could see of him anyway) were ruined every time he opened his mouth. I felt bad for whoever had to put up with him on a daily basis.

But even his foul behavior couldn't completely erase the memory of the sound of his voice and the way he rolled that lollipop around in his mouth. And the soft feel of his hands against my leg...

In one swift movement, I turned the water onto cold and blasted myself with frigid spray. Fantasizing about some man I literally met on the side of the road wasn't going to happen. Men were off-limits to me. Period.

As if to punctuate my declaration further, I shut off the spray and began to dry off. The whole time I worked on my hair, I thought about the view I was missing. I laid down the comb with a frustrated sigh. My eyes noticed something on the counter.

A pair of scissors.

I glanced up at the wet blond hair hanging limply over my shoulders. I was tired of feeling heavy. I was tired of wearing my hair the way other people wanted me to wear it. I was going to be like the sun. I was going to embrace the new day.

I pulled my hair back into a low ponytail at the base of my neck and slid the band down a couple inches.

And then I chopped it off.

When I pulled my hand away, about six inches of hair bound together with a black tie came with it. I tossed it in the nearby trashcan and looked up. My hair hung above my shoulders now, some of the newly cut ends flipping outward. I ran my fingers through it with a smile. I felt lighter already.

Feeling empowered, I combed the front down over my face and cut in very long bangs. In fact, they were so long, I didn't know if they even were bangs or just a long layer. I wasn't a hair stylist. In fact, I was pretty sure I'd lost my ever-loving mind, but I didn't care.

After I was done, I cleaned up the hair that had fallen in the sink and then worked a little mousse through the strands. I applied a layer of sunblock before standing back to study my handiwork. Not bad. It appeared even because I used the hair tie as a guide. The real test would be once it was dry.

I wasn't about to blow-dry it. I wanted to get outside and enjoy the colors in the sky before the sun rose so high it was only blue.

In the kitchen, I rummaged for coffee, only to find there wasn't any. What kind of human being had no coffee? A trip to the store would be a must later today. There was a little OJ in the fridge so I settled for that and carried it toward the back door.

On the way, Salty stared at me hatefully. I guess my fresh appearance didn't make me any more likable.

As soon as I opened the sliding door, fresh sea air greeted me and I took a deep breath. I stepped out, my bare foot meeting the textured wood of the deck. Before I could fully step outside, Salty (aka Demon) shot out the door between my legs with an angry growl.

I stumbled and almost fell over from the stupid animal but caught myself just in time. As I straightened, the stupid cat leapt off the deck railing and into the sand dune.

Did I mention people were not allowed on the dunes? They weren't. It was actually a law here, and if caught, you would be fined heavily.

"Salty!" I yelled. "Get back here!"

Aunt Ruth was more than happy to let me stay at her place while she recovered from surgery with Claire's parents. She even refused to take rent money.

The only thing she asked was that I feed Salty and take care of him. Her indoor cat. I hadn't even been here a full day and already he was running off outside where he wasn't supposed to be.

Hey, Aunt Ruth, thanks for letting me borrow your beach house. You know that cat you love so much? I lost him.

Yeah, that was *not* a conversation I wanted to have.

I set down the glass and leaned over the railing. Salty was sitting calmly below, looking up at me with a haughty expression. Almost as if he were mocking me.

"Don't think I won't come down there!" I bellowed.

He just sat there.

"No tuna for you!" I threatened.

Nothing.

"Fine!" I shouted and began climbing over the railing. I felt a splinter ram its way into my palm and I bit my lip, thinking of all the ways I was going to make this demon suffer for this. Once I was on the outside of the deck, I looked down.

Whoa.

That was a lot bigger jump than I realized.

"Stupid cat!" I snapped.

Salty hissed and ran off.

"Wait!" I yelled and squeezed my eyes shut before jumping off. I landed on my feet, immediately falling onto my butt. The sand here was cold because it was mostly shaded. Salty was close by, and I reached out to grab him.

He avoided my grasp and took off running, this time toward the beach. Was he insane? Cats didn't like the beach. Did they?

I scrambled up and went chasing after him, yelling his name the entire way. Right next door to Ruth's house was another house right on the beach. The distance between the homes wasn't very far, and in between them where the dune gave way to the beach was a very tall wooden pole with a light on the top.

It was this light pole that Salty decided to climb.

I scurried over the dune and skidded to a stop beneath the light post. The good news was Salty had enough sense not to climb to the top. The bad news was he was high enough that I couldn't reach him.

"You're evil!" I hissed at him.

He hissed back.

"Come down here, right now!" I demanded, looking around for some sort of stick or something I might be able to poke him down with.

He didn't listen and there were no sticks lying around. I was going to have to go up there and get him. The large, brown pole was literally a cylinder shape of wood sticking up out of the ground. There was no ladder on the side, nothing for me to use as foot holds.

I tested out the width of the wood by wrapping my arms around it. My hands didn't meet so it was fairly large. I backed up a few steps and took a running leap at it. The plan was to jump on it and, using my arms and legs, wrap myself around it and then shimmy up.

Yeah, that didn't happen. I bounced off like I was a basketball thrown in a lousy shot. With an oomph, I landed on my back in the sand.

I stared up at the blue, cloudless sky. How in the hell did these things happen to me?

Taking a different approach, I wrapped my arms and legs around the pole and then tried to climb it that way.

Can I just say I learned two things:

1. I hated cats.

2. I had no idea how strippers "worked" a pole because it wasn't easy.

I released the pole and stood staring up at the cat. He gave me a pitiful meow, and I rolled my eyes. "Sure, now you want my pity."

There was really only one thing to do. Call the fire department. Maybe they would send out some hot, muscle-bound guy with a ladder that I could ogle as he saved the day.

"Ha!" I told the cat. "Who has the last laugh now?"

I turned away, toward my house to get my cell phone. I heard the sound of a slamming door, but I didn't bother to turn and look.

"What the hell is going on out here!" roared a vaguely familiar voice.

I stopped in the sand.

It couldn't be...

"Who the hell are you?" he roared.

I spun on my heel.

Blond hair flopped into his eyes, unshaven jaw, chiseled cheekbones, hulking shape...

It was the guy from last night.

I could only pray he didn't recognize me.

"My cat is stuck." I pointed up at Salty. "I was just going to call the fire department."

"You just can't stay out of trouble, can you?" He crossed his arms over his very broad chest. His very naked, smooth chest.

Holy suntanned muscles.

So much for him not remembering me. "It's not my fault he raced up that pole like some circus act."

"He was no doubt trying to get away from you," he muttered, staring up at Salty. Then he looked back at me. "That's *your* cat?" he asked, his voice filled with doubt.

"It's my Aunt Ruth's cat." I clarified. He didn't need to know she wasn't my aunt. "I'm housesitting for her."

"You're living next door?" He said it like it was the most annoying thing in the world.

"I'm just visiting."

"Yeah?" He sauntered over toward me. The wind off the water blew around us, ruffling the blond hair around his head, and I couldn't help but notice the way the muscles in his very well-defined chest shifted as he moved.

Instead of staring at his rock-hard body, I looked at his face, taking in the features I wasn't able to see last night.

His eyes were blue. Like a deep ocean blue. His skin was tan, the kind of tan one only got from living at the beach, and judging from the lightness of his eyebrows, he was a natural blond. He looked like he was born and raised in the sand. His skin was smooth and his biceps were round and solid.

He drew closer, towering over me like he was some giant and I was his dinner. Those beautiful blue eyes were narrowed and from this distance, I could see they were slightly bloodshot.

Maybe he was an alcoholic. But weren't alcoholics friendly?

"Let me fill you in on how things work around here," he said, stopping so we were practically toe-to-toe.

His breath didn't smell like alcohol. It smelled like coffee. The big, fat jerk had coffee and I didn't.

"This is a quiet stretch of sand. All the people in this area live here, year round. We mind our own business. We stay out of each other's way. We definitely do not let our cats loose and then come out on the sand at the crack of dawn, bellowing like some kind of crazy person."

"What are you, like, the beach police?" I retorted. I held up a hand. "No wait, I know. You're neighborhood watch." I couldn't help it. I giggled.

Judging from the dark scowl on his face, he wasn't amused.

I sighed, he was totally ruining my whole "new day" approach to life this morning. "I have no intention of disturbing your peace. It's the reason I'm here too. I'll just call the fire department, get my cat, and we won't have to see each other ever again."

I spun to go inside and get my phone. Just like last night, he stopped me. This time, instead of taking my wrist, he palmed my hand, pulling me back around. I yelped and pulled my hand away, shaking it a little as if to get rid of the pain.

"What's wrong with your hand?" he asked, his voice losing some of its annoyed, sarcastic edge.

"Nothing." I sniffed, tucking it beneath my other arm against my side.

"I didn't mean to hurt you." He ran a hand through his blond hair, pushing it away from his face. Damn, his eyes were blue.

"It's okay."

Carefully, he reached out and pulled my hand away, to hold it out between us. In the fleshy part of my palm under my thumb was an angry-looking splinter. The skin was red around the edges and slightly puffy. In the center you could see the sliver of wood buried in my skin.

"It's just a splinter," I told him, trying to pull my hand away. "Demon cat - three, Talie - zero."

"Demon cat?" he mused, the corner of his lip lifting. He had full lips, the kind that were good for biting.

It took me a moment to answer because he was cradling my hand in his while smoothing his thumb around the area where the splinter was. His touch was beyond gentle yet self-assured, like he knew what he was doing. Little prickles of pleasure raced up and down my legs because even just that slight touch from him was so very good.

I cleared my throat. "That cat hates me."

That statement earned me a full-on grin. His straight, white teeth flashed, and a dimple appeared in his chin. From this close up, I could see the roughness of the stubble growing along his jaw. Out here in the sun, it looked golden, as if to highlight his already perfect face.

The cat made a pitiful sound and I looked up. "I better go."

I tugged my hand back and he let go, turning around to walk away. But he didn't go back up the steps to his deck. Instead, he leapt onto the pole and started to climb. It was just unfair he could do that and I couldn't.

I expected Salty to react to him the same way he did me. Yeah, no. He gave another pitiful meow and allowed the man to lift him up and perch him on his shoulder like a parrot. Seconds later, he was striding back across the sand to me, with a happy-looking Salty.

"Thank you," I said, reaching out for the cat.

He hissed and growled.

I snatched my hand back and scowled. "See!"

He chuckled. The sound brushed over my body, setting it to tingle. "I'll carry him."

I led him onto the deck and toward the sliding door, which was still open. My OJ was sitting forgotten on the arm of a lounge chair. I pushed the door open a little wider and turned to get the cat, but he was much closer than I expected. I collided with his chest and the cat. He reached out to steady me and rolled his eyes.

"You are a disaster."

"Gee, thanks."

He stepped around me to put Salty on the floor, who immediately ran off into Ruth's bedroom. I hoped he hid there the rest of the day.

"So do you have a name?" I asked. "Or should I just keep thinking of you as the rude guy next door."

"Gavin," he supplied. "You're Talie?"

I nodded. "Well, thanks, Gavin," I said, trying out his name on my tongue. "I won't disturb your peace anymore."

"Somehow I don't believe that."

I made a shooing motion with my hand, hoping he would get the point. He grabbed the hand with the splinter and said, "You need to get that out before it gets infected."

"Will do."

Instead of taking me for my word, he slid the door shut behind him and then towed me along into the bathroom.

"What the hell are you doing?"

"I'm getting this out."

"I can manage."

He barked a laugh. "No, you can't."

I really didn't like being treated like some child who had no clue. I was a grown woman. I could take care of myself.

I spun around to rush out of the room, but he caught me around the waist and lifted me off my feet like I weighed nothing more than a seashell.

"Hey!" I gasped.

My bottom hit the bathroom counter and he stepped between my legs. I lost the ability to think. I glanced down at the way my pale knees looked framing out his tight, toned waist. My heart started to pound as I glanced at the board shorts he wore. They hung low, exposing a deep V shape low on his waist. I didn't know what those lines were called, but I had a serious hot flash thinking about licking them.

Gavin seemed completely unaffected by my closeness as he opened up the medicine cabinet beside my head and withdrew a pair of tweezers.

"I'll do this," I said, trying to take them.

"Shh," he shushed. "I know what I'm doing."

"Oh, so you're an expert splinter remover?"

His eyes flashed up to mine. "I'm an expert at a lot of things."

Oh my.

Did I mention I hadn't had sex in six months? It was this moment when my body decided to remind me of that and how utterly sexy this man was.

No! I told myself. *No, no, no.*

"Don't fidget," he said, palming my hips and stilling my body. I hadn't even realized I was moving.

He lifted my hand and turned it palm up. Then he pinched the skin with one hand (which hurt really bad!) and used the tweezers to pluck out the splinter. He got it in one try.

He held it up between us and I noted it had some blood on the end.

"Ow," I said.

He smiled.

My stomach fluttered uncontrollably. "Thanks."

"Might want to wash that off," he said, motioning toward it. There was a small bead of blood welling in the center.

I hopped down off the counter and washed my hands, ignoring the sting. When I was done, I glanced in the mirror. My hair was almost completely dry, and despite being outside on the windy beach, it wasn't a knotted mess.

Instead, it waved around my head naturally tousled and beach ready. A few of the ends were still flipping out, but it appeared they were styled to do just that. My cheeks were flushed and Gavin was the reason.

My eyes met his in the mirror. We stared at each other for one long, charged second. Suddenly, this bathroom seemed too small. The sparks between us were so tangible it felt as if we couldn't all fit in this space. Overwhelming energy burst around us, and a fine tremor started in my hands.

"I'm going to go," he said, breaking our eye contact first.

I nodded without moving. He left without delay, almost like he was running and couldn't get out fast enough.

I didn't bother to chase him down.

I was too shocked to move.

10

Talie

Two days later, I got up with the sunrise to walk along the sand. All the best seashells could be found early, as the tide was just going out.

I was hoping to find a shark tooth. Not the ones that everybody finds, the small black ones with the sharp end and jagged side. Those seemed like a dime a dozen. I wanted to find a truly remarkable one. As big as my palm, something that showed me just how big the world out there was.

Before heading outside, I dressed in a navy-blue tankini with a plunging neckline (Claire said if I refused to wear a bikini, the tankini had to be sexy) with turquoise trim. I added a thin, white linen cover-up dress with a rope tie around the middle and grabbed a large-brimmed turquoise hat to keep the sun off my face.

Salty and I had settled in a hate-hate relationship that included me feeding him and him showing me his displeasure before running off to hide for most the day. The last thing I did was put on a pot of coffee to brew so the rich, dark wake-me-up in a cup was ready when I got back.

Outside, the sun was low in the sky, white, puffy clouds were tinted pink, and overhead the sky was already a brilliant blue. The sound of ocean waves crashing against the shore was like music to my ears. It was so loud it drowned out most of my thoughts. And the ones that were most persistent, the thoughts that threatened to bring down my mood? I let the breeze carry them behind me to be lost out to sea.

I wandered down the beach, peeking up at Gavin's beach house as I walked past. It was a blue house with white shutters. It looked very similar to Aunt Ruth's, but it appeared bigger. Propped against the back sliders was a large surfboard. An image of him wet and glistening atop a board in the center of the deep sea made my stomach flip over.

The guy was an ass, but damn he was sexy. He made my pulse race in ways I'd never experienced. And it was hard not to replay the splinter scene over and over again in my head. How one moment he could be acting like a first-class mule and the next touch me with such gentleness was a puzzle. If I wasn't careful, he'd give me a serious case of whiplash.

Not that I was going to see him again. The way he'd left so abruptly the other day and then not resurfaced from inside his house since was proof of that.

Not that I was looking out the window or watching his house from my deck or anything.

That would just be stalker-ish.

I turned my attention back to the task at hand: splashing my feet in the surf, clearing my head, and searching for shells and shark teeth. The last thing I needed to think about was some guy. That would only just get me hurt again.

Claire said Blake called looking for me the day before. She told him I wasn't home and she'd give me the message when I got back. He was going to be waiting a while before I got back. I snickered to myself as I picked up a beautiful white shell.

Joanna tried to call me once as well, but I let the call go to voicemail. I walked into a long stretch of shells and I forgot everything except the feeling of the sand between my toes and the wind in my hair.

I didn't find the shark tooth I was hoping for, but I found many other beautiful shells, so many that I had to use the end of my dress as a makeshift bucket to hold them.

The sun was much higher in the sky when I wandered back toward the beach house. The wind seemed to be stronger than earlier and the tide wasn't as low as before.

I was wading through the water when my toe struck something in the surf. The water rushed out, making me feel like it was going to tug me into its depths as it went, and I saw the rounded top of a conch shell. It looked fully intact, and excitement skittered through me.

I released the hold I had on my hat and bent to retrieve it just as a strong gust of wind whipped by, lifting the hat up off my head and sending it backward.

I let it go, instead keeping my grip on the shell as a wave crashed practically on top of me and pushed me over. I shrieked and fell sideways, taking in a mouthful of salty water. I sputtered and pushed myself up, grappling for the ends of my dress that held all my treasures.

I managed to catch most, only losing a few. Dripping wet and tasting nothing but salt, I rushed ashore before another wave could push me over.

I wasn't watching where I was running and I hit a solid wall and bounced back. Before I could fall again, two hands reached out to steady me. "Most people take off their clothes to take a swim," Gavin quipped.

Still holding the ends of my dress with one hand, I pushed the saturated ends of my hair away from my face. "Ha-ha."

"You lose something?" He held up my hat.

"What are you doing out here?" I asked and took the hat, dumping all of my shells into it, and then let my cover-up fall back into place.

"I live here." He spread his arms, gesturing to the beach. The action drew all of my attention to his body. I didn't think he ever wore a shirt. Once again, he was wearing dangerously low-slung board shorts. The fabric was wet from the water and the added weight dragged them down until I could see the area leading toward his most manly place and how the skin there wasn't as tan as the rest of him. There was no trail of hair like Blake had. Gavin was completely hairless and smooth. I bit my lip, wondering if he was as cleanly groomed beneath his shorts as he was everywhere else.

"Talie?" I heard him say, but his voice was far away. My attention was seriously diverted to other places. His abs were lean and cut. It was definitely obvious he spent time surfing because his body showed off the work. His skin was damp and glistened slightly beneath the early morning sun.

"I didn't think you ever came out of your house," I replied and then wanted to kick myself.

He lifted his eyebrows. "You've been watching for me?"

I felt my cheeks burn with embarrassment. *Idiot*, I told myself. "Of course not," I snapped. "I was just noticing how peaceful the last couple days had been and the fact that you *weren't* in them."

"I'm out here every morning to surf. You've just not noticed me until today."

"So you've been watching me?" I said, smug.

He grinned and didn't bother to deny it. My entire body flushed. The fact that he watched me meant he liked what he saw... right?

"That hat of yours is like a neon sign. It's kind of hard not to notice."

So much for thinking he might like the way I looked. *Bummer.* Yes, I know. I said I wasn't going to worry about a guy. But that didn't mean I didn't want him to enjoy the way I looked.

"It's not that bright," I muttered and looked away, back into the water. Surprisingly, the conch shell was still there, the water parting over it as it moved.

"Hold this," I said and pushed the hat containing all my shells into his arms.

"Would love to," he said dryly as I waded back into the water to retrieve the shell. I'd never found a whole conch before and I really wanted to get it.

The shell was partially buried in the wet sand, which was the reason it hadn't washed away yet. Because the bottom was open, it acted like a suction cup against the packed wet sand. Bending at the waist, I plunged both my hands into the cool, brackish water and tugged. It didn't lift on my first try, and of course, another wave crashed right where I was standing. This time I braced myself and didn't fall over, but I did stand there for a long moment waiting for some of the water to drain away. As it did, the surf rushed around my arms and legs, spraying me with water drops.

The sensation of rushing water was interrupted.

A sharp, stabbing pain followed by an intense burning, kind of like my arm was on fire, made me cry out. I jerked back to get away from whatever was hurting me, and I caught a glimpse of a large jellyfish being tugged away by a wave.

I stumbled backward, the pain fairly intense, as my brain processed the fact I was just stung by the creature.

Just as I was about to fall, a pair of warm, solid arms wrapped around me from behind. I took immediate advantage of his nearness and leaned against him, giving all my weight for him to support.

"What happened?" Gavin said against my ear.

"I think a jellyfish just stung me," I said, my voice low and strained. The burning and stinging was very intense. It hurt a lot more than I thought a sting like this would.

"Only you would find an angry jellyfish," he rumbled.

"Hey—" I started to argue, but the words fell away. I was in pain, damn it.

"Where did it get you?"

I raised my arm to inspect the spot where it burned. There was a large, bright-red welt and a rash spreading down around my wrist. In the center of the reddest area, something was sticking out. I freaked out and began waving my arm. "Get it off!" I screeched. "Get it off me!"

"Talie," he said firmly, interrupting my meltdown. How could he be so calm? "It's the tentacle. It stuck to your skin when he got you."

"I don't want it there."

He chuckled. "I got that."

I started at it with my fingers to yank that sucker out, but he stopped me. "That's just going to hurt worse."

I glared at him. Gavin tucked my hat with the shells in it under his arm and then reached for me. He lifted me easily, swung me up into his arms and cradled me against his chest.

"What the hell are you doing?" I demanded.

Secretly, I freaking loved the feeling of him carrying me as if I weighed nothing at all.

"Do you know first aid for a jellyfish sting?" He stared down at me. The deep azure penetrated me down to my very core.

I shook my head.

"Well, I do."

With that he set off across the sand, passing by the surfboard lying near the wooden stairs, and began climbing them without even breathing heavy.

I blinked past the burn in my arm and looked up at the familiar sight of the white house with blue shutters. It drew closer the more he walked.

He was taking me to his house.

11

Talie

He carried me to the couch, which wasn't far
from the doors off the deck. He walked with ease and
grace, barely jostling me or needing to shift my weight
in his arms. His skin felt like a satin sheet that was just
plucked from the dryer. It seemed unfair a man would
have such soft skin, but I couldn't bring myself to be
jealous.

Especially not when I was currently enjoying the
way he felt against me. It seemed the sting on my arm
was hurting worse; none of the pain dissipated. It hurt
and the pain was distracting me from true admiration
of the feel of being against him.

Before he laid me on the couch, I let my cheek
fall against his shoulder, allowing my eyes to flutter
closed for just a moment and just let myself be held.
It wasn't like he was holding me because he loved me,
or even that he cared about me. Hell, I was pretty
sure he didn't even like me. I wasn't even sure I liked
him.

But being in his arms just now, I was comfortable. I was safe. And honestly, just like cutting my hair and watching the sunrise, being in Gavin's arms was somewhat freeing.

After a few minutes of relaxing against him, of taking comfort in his hold, I realized he wasn't walking anymore. He was standing stock still, unmoving... almost like he was paralyzed.

I lifted my head and looked up. Our eyes collided.

He was watching me.

Intense azure eyes stared down, and he wore an unreadable expression. His jaw was tight and his lips drew downward. Suddenly, I was extremely embarrassed. I was practically curling up against him like a purring cat. He probably thought I was some psycho who would steal one of his shirts on the way out the door and sleep in it.

"Sorry," I said, unable to tear my gaze away from his. "It hurts pretty bad."

So what if I sounded like a big weenie? I would rather sound like a wimp than some pathetic woman who was starved for attention.

Oh. My. God. Was I?

Was I so lacking in any kind of physical affection that I was now turning a situation where a man was merely trying to help an injured woman into something more?

The muscle in the side of his jaw ticked, and I bit back a grimace.

Time to get it together, Talie. I could analyze myself and behavior later. Alone.

Cambria Hebert

Gavin lowered me to the cushions, laying me across the plush, oversized couch and then propping a pillow behind my back.

"I'm fine," I said and started to sit up. "I can just go have this looked at in Surf City at the walk-in clinic."

"You're going to drive yourself over there with a jellyfish tentacle in your arm?"

Well, duh. Of course I would.

"No," he commanded.

Did he think I was a dog?

"You're not the boss of me!" I snapped like an angry five-year-old and swung my feet onto the floor.

His arms shot out, caging me in against the couch. He leaned close, so close I could feel the coolness of his breath across my cheek. "You wouldn't make it three steps toward the door."

"What are you gonna do? Tie me down?"

"If I have to," he rumbled.

I shuddered. The image of him tying me up and doing whatever he pleased with me sent jolts of heady desire down low into my belly.

His lips curved into a knowing smile. "You'd like that, wouldn't you?"

I gave him a *hell no* look.

"Little liar," he whispered before pulling away.

I sank back against the cushions, my body feeling like a bowl full of Jell-O. Twinges of pain shot up my arm, and I looked down. My wrist and forearm were swelling slightly and my skin was an angry shade of red.

"Could I have some ice?" I asked, thinking it would soothe the pain.

"No," he said on his way out of the room.

That was just rude.

He was entirely too bossy.

"What the hell did you bring me here for if you weren't going to give me some ice?" I yelled after him.

He didn't even reply. A few moments later, he came sauntering back into the room, carrying a load of supplies. None of it appeared to be ice. He was still not wearing a shirt, and frankly, looking at all his tan perfection was making me grouchy. He shouldn't put the goods on display if he wasn't going to let me sample them.

"Don't you ever wear a shirt?" I grumped.

"Only when I have to." He was busy lining up supplies along the wooden coffee table.

"What is all that?" I asked dubiously.

He picked up a pair of rubber gloves and slid them on. "Stuff to treat you."

"I need ice. Not…" I glanced at the large clear bottle with a white label. "Is that vinegar?"

"Yes," he said calmly. "Ice will change the toxicity in the sting and cause more pain. Vinegar will neutralize some of the proteins and make it feel better."

Well, didn't he sound intelligent?

As he was opening up a little white kit, he glanced at me, his eyes assessing my face. "Are you feeling dizzy? Trouble breathing?"

"No."

"That's good," he said and smiled. His voice was low and soothing. He was calm and collected and acted like he treated these kinds of stings all the time. It made me feel safe.

He held up a pair of large tweezers in his gloved hand. "I'm going to remove the tentacle. I'll be as gentle as I can, okay? Try and hold still."

I held out my arm to him and turned my face away.

He chuckled. "Chicken."

"I'm sorry, but I don't want to watch you dig that thing out of my skin."

I felt a small pinch and the burning intensified, and then he pulled away. "Got it," he said.

I watched as he wrapped the nasty thing in a napkin and then slid off his glove and created a ball around the napkin. Next he handed me a large plastic bowl. "Hold this under your arm," he instructed.

I did and he began to pour the vinegar over the wound. I held my breath, expecting more pain, but nothing happened. When he was done, he took the bowl and soaked a thick white cloth in the leftover vinegar. Then he placed it over my arm.

"It needs to soak for a few minutes."

I wrinkled my nose against the strong odor of the liquid and settled against the couch.

"Want some coffee?" he called from what I guessed was the kitchen.

"Sure."

He returned a few moments later carrying two white mugs. They looked small in his large hands. I took the offered mug and took a sip of the brew and groaned appreciatively.

I felt the intensity of his stare and glanced over, suddenly feeling uncomfortable. He was staring, staring in a way that made me aware... aware of his attraction.

It wasn't one-sided, all those thoughts I'd been having. He'd had a few too.

"If I just need to soak this in vinegar, I can do it at my place," I said, starting to sit up.

He didn't say anything, just watched me over the rim of his cup and took a long swallow. When he was done, he set it aside and stood, coming to sit on the coffee table directly in front of me.

He lifted my arm and removed the cloth. After studying it for a few minutes, he picked up a credit card. "I'm going to scrape the top of the sting. It might hurt." He took no pleasure in that thought, which made my insides do a little happy dance.

"You want to scrape my arm with your credit card?"

"I'll be gentle," he said, looking me in the eye. "It's to remove any leftover nematocysts."

I bit my lip and nodded.

Surprisingly, it didn't hurt. If anything, it felt good. The area was beginning to itch and this was good relief. After a few seconds of scraping the top, he reapplied the vinegar compress.

"After a few minutes, we'll wash it off and apply some hydrocortisone cream."

"Thank you," I said, meaning it. He sure knew how to act like a jerk, but it was clear he knew how to not act like one too.

"So," I said after a couple minutes of silence. "What do you do?"

"Surf."

"Oh. Are you a pro?"

"Nope."

"Do you live here alone?"

"Yep." He moved off the coffee table and went into the kitchen. I heard some cupboards opening and closing, and a few seconds later, he came back shoving a little white cake in his mouth. A rectangular white box was tucked under his arm and he carried a clear wrapper with another identical cake inside.

He sat down and shoved the other one in his mouth. Whole.

"Snack cake?" he said, offering me the box as he propped his bare feet on the table.

"No, thanks."

He shrugged and pulled out another package and proceeded to make short work of it as well.

I took his obvious preoccupation with Little Debbie to study my surroundings. Now that my arm wasn't hurting as badly, I could concentrate on his house.

It was minimalistic and simple. The living room and dining room were one open space. It consisted of a tan couch, two club chairs, and a coffee table in the center.

Adjacent from the couch was a large flat-screen hanging on the wall with a small narrow table beneath it. The top of the table had what I assumed were empty boxes of snack cakes.

The coffee table also boasted a few empty boxes of the junk.

I thought he might have a problem.

"So what's your favorite snack cake?" I asked.

"I don't discriminate," he said, lowering the box and picking up his coffee.

"Do you eat anything besides snack cakes?" I wondered out loud.

"Of course."

He was a man of few words. It seemed the only conversation he knew how to have was an argument.

After a few more silent moments, I sat up. "I should go. I know you probably have things to do." I really didn't think he had anything to do, but I didn't know what else to say.

He stood swiftly and sat down in front of me again. Our bare knees brushed together and a jolt of electricity moved through him and into me. I gasped a little in surprise.

He didn't acknowledge what I knew he felt. Gavin discarded the cloth and patted the area dry with another towel. "How's it feel?"

"Better," I stuttered. The steady rise and fall of his shoulders while he breathed was hypnotizing. And the way he smelled made me want to lean closer. He smelled like the beach—you know, that kind of oil that you use to help you tan? Like coconuts and sunshine.

I watched as Gavin uncapped a tube of hydrocortisone and squeezed some out on his fingers. He laid my arm across his lap, my hand falling just beside his hip.

Dear God, I was inches from his cock.

He took his time rubbing the little bit of cream over the injury. Moisture gathered in my bathing suit bottom and my breasts began to ache with desire.

"Why are you here, Talie?" he asked, no longer rubbing the medicine in, but not releasing my arm.

"Because a jellyfish stung me?"

The side of his lip tilted, and I wanted so badly to lean over and kiss the corner of his mouth. "I meant here, on the island."

"Oh. Right."

He began to draw lazy circles over the inside of my elbow with his fingers. He didn't play fair. How was I supposed to keep up with a conversation when he did things like that?

And why did he affect me this way?

He was maddening, bossy, and he lived off snack cakes for goodness sake.

"Talie?" he said, my name ripping from deep within his throat.

"Oh, um... Vacation."

"Who takes a vacation alone?"

"Who lives in a beach house alone?" I answered.

"I like my privacy. I'm not a social guy."

"Then why did you bring me here?"

"I don't know," he said, sounding absolutely mystified.

"I'll go," I declared.

He nodded.

Neither of us moved. He didn't release my arm.

It was as if we were both paralyzed in a bubble of attraction. The pull between us was so unlike anything I'd ever experienced before. It was physically powerful, chaining us together where we sat. Both of us voiced the intent to break apart, to go our separate ways, but our bodies overruled our brains.

There would be no moving away.

Only closer.

In one fluid movement, Gavin came forward, sweeping an arm around my waist and pulling me to the very edge of the couch. His knees parted and my body fit between them as his lips fastened to mine.

We were Velcro. He was the rough side and I was the soft. The closer he pressed, the more tightly we fused. I swear to you in that moment I didn't think. I couldn't. I could only be pummeled by the onslaught of heavy desire that flooded my system like a surging waterway.

Gavin's fingers delved into the hair at the base of my neck, tangling around the blond strands and pushing my head even closer. Our teeth bumped together and he opened even wider, slipping his tongue inside my mouth, smoothing over the edges of my teeth and stroking the roof of my mouth.

I melted in his embrace. The heat from his skin, the taste of his kiss… intoxicating was an understatement. He was the most potent drug, the kind that just one hit would kill, and I was well on my way toward death. And I didn't care. In that moment, the way our mouths moved together was so intense I would have gladly given my life for just a few more minutes.

My fingernails dug into the bulging muscles in his biceps, like I was on some kind of carnival ride and needed to hang on for dear life. My lungs burned with the need for oxygen, but breathing would require lifting my head, and that was something I couldn't stand.

The kiss went on and on. It was moist and hot. Gavin allowed my tongue to explore every place it wandered, and every groan that escaped my throat he captured and added it to his own.

Just when I thought my chest might burst, he pulled away. My lips felt swollen and the air that rushed between us felt cool against my overheated skin. I stared up at him dumbly, completely at a loss for words.

No one had ever kissed me like that.

No one had ever drawn out that kind of response with just a single kiss.

I know he saw shock in my eyes. It reverberated through my bones. I took a deep, unsteady breath and my breasts brushed against his shirtless chest.

"I changed my mind," he said, his voice made of gravel.

"What?" I asked, breathless and totally confused.

His cobalt eyes fastened on mine. "I don't want you to go." The hand still tangled in my hair tightened, as if he expected me to refuse.

Refusing was not an option.

Surrender was my only choice.

All I could manage was a single word.

"Yes."

12

Talie

His touch was like fire. Tomorrow, I would likely have blisters from the flames his fingers left behind. After my single-word answer, we didn't speak again. Our lips and hands did all the talking.

His body was smooth like polished granite, and his tropical scent enthralled my senses so the only thing that existed was him. Gavin knew exactly where to touch, exactly the right amount of pressure to apply when he dragged his fingertips down the base of my neck and delved below the neckline of the cover-up I wore.

My breasts tingled with need. The flesh felt swollen as blood and desire filled them, hoping one of Gavin's magic hands would come their way. My nipples were drawn so taut it was almost painful, and every time I shifted, they brushed against the material of my bathing suit, the friction only whipping me into more of a frenzy.

I was bold in my exploration of his body. I wasn't the kind of girl to shy away. I was hungry—

starving actually—and my body instinctively knew he would satiate that hunger like no one else could.

One of my hands cupped his pec, squeezing and then pinching the nipple until it puckered tightly. He groaned and I swept my other hand up into the thick blond hair, kneading my fingertips into his scalp.

The burning of the sting on my wrist intensified when the soft strands of his hair brushed against the injury. It was enough to break through the haze of passion and caused me to suck in a breath.

"Easy," he said against my lips, standing up and pulling me along with him. He was so tall he towered over me, the height difference between us staggering. I only came to his chest, and as we stood, I had to crane my head back to look up at him.

Very carefully, Gavin reached up and took my hand from his hair. He brought it down so my arm rested against his shoulder. "Probably shouldn't move that too much," he said, allowing his fingers to lightly trail down my arm to the underside of my armpit and then down along the side of my breast. I bit my lip to keep from sighing with pleasure.

"I want to touch you," I said brazenly.

He smiled smugly as he bent at the knees to lower himself down a little closer to my level. "Good thing you've got two hands."

His lips claimed mine again and our tongues melted together like an ice cream sundae on a summer day. Even melted, it tasted damn good.

My uninjured arm traveled down and my fingers played with the edges of his shorts. Dipping my fingertips beneath the damp fabric, I scraped my nails over the side of his hip and he groaned. Both his arms swept around me, yanking me off my feet so I was completely plastered against his front. As he deepened the kiss, his hips tilted toward me.

His need could not be denied. His thick, hard length pushed insistently against my lower abdomen, and the area beneath my bikini bottom began to throb. In one swift movement, Gavin tucked me beneath him, spreading out my body on the oversized couch like I was a buffet and he hadn't eaten in a week. He lowered his body on top of mine, reaching around behind us to grab my leg and wrap it around his hip.

From there, he lowered himself and I gasped. His rigid cock pressed exactly into my core. My knees started to shake and a fine tremor vibrated my body. He dry-humped me with finesse until my entire lower half trembled so badly I had trouble keeping my leg up around his hip. Oh God, the rhythm in which he moved was my body's favorite song. With each thrust, he lingered a little bit longer so his entire considerable length rubbed against my engorged, needy clit.

With a moan, my hands fell to my sides and I arched up off the couch, my head thrown back. Gavin's mouth immediately fastened on one of my nipples and sucked with fortitude. My bathing suit and cover-up became wet from his ministrations.

"Oh yes," I purred, holding his head there just a little bit longer.

His chuckle vibrated my flesh, and I groaned.

"Do you like this?" he asked, pulling away to sit between my legs. His fingers held my cover-up.

"Yes."

"Too bad," he growled and ripped the fabric right off my body. "It's in my way."

Cambria Hebert

The string that tied the halter-top around my neck was quickly pulled, and he shoved the top down around my waist, completely baring my breasts.

Without a second to spare, he took one in his hand, kneading the sides while diving back down and latching onto it with his lips. He used his teeth to pull at the nipple and his tongue to lap at the skin around it.

I couldn't hold still. I was like some kind of nervous virgin. My entire body shook like I was my own personal earthquake.

Gavin looked up at me, his eyes dark navy pools, and smiled a wolfish smile.

"More," I demanded.

He licked down my belly and used his teeth to pull the string on the side of my bathing suit bottom, tearing the fabric away and throwing it over the side of the couch. He pushed one of my legs over the back of the sofa and then pushed the other one so far open that my foot rested on the coffee table.

"Stay open for me," he growled and lowered his mouth.

Oh. My. Goodness. His tongue had a master's in vagina-ology. I'm pretty sure I embarrassed myself with the cries that came out of my mouth, but I scarcely heard them. His tongue was thick and wide; he could lick my entire slit with one great swipe of its textured pink surface. And sometimes he would start low, down below my opening, and drag his tongue upward, twirl around my swollen clit, and then plunge the tip into my pink, wet depths, and I would literally quake with satisfaction.

When he sat up between my knees, his lips glistened with the juices he cajoled my body to produce, and I watched as he swiped his thumb along the wetness and then sucked it into his mouth like he wanted every last drop of me.

His eyes were heavy lidded when he reached for the tie on his shorts. Before releasing the part of him I most anticipated, he paused and glanced up.

"Will you let me in?"

He could have asked me to stab myself and I probably would have acquiesced. "Please," I said, my voice weak and low.

With a single tug, the strings came loose and his shorts fell open. His quivering cock sprang out, pointing at me like he was a compass and I was the destination.

He was well-endowed, so well that I had a moment of unease, wondering how all of that was going to fit inside my body. But then he pushed the shorts completely away and I was left to stare at his fully naked body. I was right; he was hairless down there. Completely smooth and pink.

Gavin grabbed his cock, starting at the base, and stroked it all the way to the tip, and I couldn't help but stare at the pearly white drop that glistened at the end. Without thinking, I pushed up and took him into my mouth, as far in as the space would allow. I sucked my way back to the tip, where I licked off that small amount of precum and swallowed it while I stared him in the eye.

"Fucking A," he said as a shudder moved up his spine.

I cupped his tight balls in my palm and released him, lowering back against the couch and spreading my legs once more. He dropped down, hands on either side of me, holding himself up, hovering above me, completely crowding my space.

Maybe he was giving me a minute to change my mind.

The world would need to end for that to happen.

I reached between us and took him in my hand. Positioning his head at my entrance, I swirled his silky skin around the lubricant my body was making by the cupful.

He tilted back his head and made a sound of appreciation. His hips surged forward and in one hard thrust, he was completely sheathed in my heat.

Gavin fell over on top of me, his body shaking with what I hoped was complete satisfaction.

"Talie," he moaned, holding himself still. Inside me, I felt the jerking of his cock as blood pumped through him.

"Wait." He groaned and slipped out.

I tried to grab him back, but he was up off the couch and disappeared in seconds. I heard a door open and close and then he reappeared carrying several foil packets.

He already had one opened and covering his length, so the others he tossed on the coffee table.

"This isn't going to be slow and gentle," he said.

"Good."

Gavin plunged into my wet depths, and I wrapped my legs around his waist like he was a wild bull and I was a cowboy. He hammered inside me, in and out, in and out. My mouth formed a silent O and pretty much stayed that way as sensation after sensation rippled over me. His breathing turned laborious and he reached down, wrapping his hand around my shoulder.

Using my body as leverage, he plunged so deep inside me that I cried out. Then he tilted his hips so his pelvic bone was fused against my crotch. Gavin rotated his hips and all the pressure of his position bore down on my clit and an orgasm like no other ripped through my body.

It was like a tornado. It spun through my body, lifting everything and flinging it aside. If I didn't have skin and bone to hold me together, there would be nothing left.

I barely registered Gavin's shout of release because I was too far gone with my own. I felt him pulsing inside me, and even though he was wearing a condom, the thought of him coming inside me was almost enough to make me orgasm again.

Blood rushed in my ears and my heart beat thundered. It took a long time for me to come back to reality. When I did, Gavin was lying on top of me, his weight pressing me into the cushions.

I reached around and squeezed his butt, just because I could.

Oh, please. You would too.

He laughed and lifted his head, resting his forehead against mine. "That was fucking awesome."

I sighed. I thought he might kiss me; I really wanted him to.

But he didn't.

Instead, he pushed up off me and got to his feet.

How could he stand already? My body was still experiencing aftershocks from what we just did.

Gavin didn't say anything, but disappeared into the bathroom again, where I heard briefly running water and a toilet flush. I sat up, looking for my bottoms and seeing them lying across the room.

He appeared, no longer naked but dressed in a pair of tight black boxer briefs. He didn't have an ounce of fat on his body. He was utterly gorgeous.

He walked around and picked up my bottoms and tossed them over the couch to me.

I quickly pulled them on, suddenly feeling self-conscious about lying there naked. After retying my top around my neck, Gavin appeared before me, reaching out to take my arm and bringing it up for him to study. The markings were still very red and the skin was puffy with a rash.

"How's this feeling?"

"Better," I said. I'm pretty sure that kind of sex would have taken away the pain from being run over by a bulldozer.

"It's going to look like this for a couple days yet."

I nodded.

Now that the intense attraction between us had been acted upon, a small amount of awkwardness descended.

I just had wild, hot, monkey sex with a stranger.

All I knew about him was that he lived on snack cakes (and how was it fair that he still looked like a freaking fitness model?) and lived at the beach.

Oh, and I knew he didn't like me.

Beyond our insane sexual chemistry, we could barely hold a conversation without arguing.

"Thanks for taking care of this," I said, pulling back my arm avoiding his stare.

"If it starts to look worse or the pain intensifies come back over here and let me see it."

He was dismissing me.

Well, that was fine. It's not like I was expecting some grand gesture. In fact, I was glad he didn't act as if we meant something to each other. We didn't.

"I'm sure it will be fine," I said, standing up and moving around him to walk toward the door.

"Talie," he called.

My heart leapt and my stomach fluttered. I turned back. "Yes?"

He came forward, his eyes like blue fire. I watched his lips, waiting for him to say something. Anything.

"Don't forget this." He held out my ruined cover-up.

I took the fabric. "Thanks."

"Sorry about ripping it."

I wanted to be mad. Not about the ruined clothes, but about something else. But I couldn't. He gave me a lopsided boyish smile, and I completely forgot about how awkward and weird this was.

"It was worth it," I retorted and winked. Then I let myself out the backdoor and walked down onto the sand.

I didn't glance back. Not because I didn't want to, but because I knew he wouldn't be standing in the window, watching me walk away.

For some reason seeing him not care I left wasn't something I wanted to observe.

13

Talie

A couple days passed peacefully. I spent time walking along the shores, browsing through the little beach shops and tanning in the sand.

Considering the awful luck I'd been having, everything was perfect.

Except for one thing.

My body turned against me. I craved him. I'd always been a fairly sexual person, enjoying the act and the pleasure that came from it. But it was as if Gavin had awakened some sort of slumbering nympho.

Almost obsessively, I thought about the time he spent inside me. Every time the breeze brushed roughly against my skin, I thought of his hands. Every time the water caressed my ankles, I thought about his mouth on my breast. When the sun would beat down on my body as I sunbathed, I thought about the heat he instilled in his kiss.

I pretty much walked around in a knot of sexual need. The problem with one-night stands was that they were only one night. It wasn't enough. One night with him was like a tease. Torture at its best. I was supposed to be here, thinking about my life, deciding where to go from here, but instead, all I could think about was how it felt to have his pulsing stiff cock inside me.

I was a slut.

A dirty ho.

I liked it.

Just as I was walking in from the beach, I heard my cell ringing on the counter. I tossed down my towel and rushed to grab it. On my way past, I saw Salty, who gave me a look that promised death later. "Don't worry," I told him. "I'll be out of here tomorrow."

"Hey," I answered breathless.

"Are you avoiding me?" Claire demanded on the other end of the line.

"Why would I be doing that?" I replied, wandering over to the fridge for a bottle of water.

"Because I've called you twice today and you haven't bothered to pick up the line!"

"Have you?" I asked, holding the phone away from my ear and glancing at the darkened screen. "I was down on the beach and left my phone in the house."

"I called a couple days ago too." She sniffed.

That was the morning I was at Gavin's. I didn't call her back because I spent the rest of that day in some kind of after-sex haze.

"Sorry. What's up?"

"Blake's looking for you."

Just the mention of his name brought down my mood. I don't know what it said about me, but this past week at the beach, I barely thought of him. It was like I didn't miss him at all. If anything, I felt slightly relieved he wasn't around. Turns out living with him was unknowingly stifling.

"Did he call you?"

"He came to the apartment."

"I'm sorry." I sighed. I really didn't think he would come looking. He was the type of guy that would want me to come back to him.

"I had to tell him that you left town," Claire said. "He wasn't happy. Not at all."

"Well, now he knows how I felt when I caught him in bed with lopsided Barbie."

"Lopsided Barbie?" she asked. I could hear the smirk in her voice.

"Never mind," I muttered. "Did you tell him where I was?"

"No. He wasn't happy about that either."

"Did he threaten you?" I asked sharply.

There was a heavy pause on the other end of the line. "No." Then she said, "Talie… Did he threaten you? Is he abusive?"

"No!" I said swiftly. "No, he's never laid a hand on me. Not that way." Blake was a lot of crappy things, but he didn't abuse me. "I just… I know how he can be when he gets angry. His reputation means everything to him."

"Yeah, I got that. I guess word got out about your separation. People are talking. His dad isn't happy."

I sighed. I was hoping it would be a while before people found out. I knew it was just wishful thinking. Raleigh wasn't a small town, but for the people who were born and raised there, it was a tightknit community.

"I'm sorry," I apologized. "I'll be home tomorrow and you won't have to deal with him again."

"You can't come home," Claire said immediately.

"What? Why not?"

"He wants you back. He even had roses. At first, I thought it was sweet, and he laid on the charm, making me think he really had thought things through and decided not to be the world's biggest douche."

The last time Blake brought me roses was almost a year ago, on his way home from some business trip. A business trip Barbie went on with him. They probably spent more time in his hotel room than working, and those stupid roses were his way of trying to make it up to me. *Jackass.*

"But you changed your mind?" I asked.

"Once he realized you weren't there and his smooth talking and flowers weren't going to score him any points, he dropped the charm. He demanded to know where you were. When I refused to tell him, he said he would find out on his own. Then he stormed out."

"I can't believe he thinks I would stay with him." I sighed. "He doesn't respect me at all, Claire."

"He acted like he owned you. Like your whereabouts was something he was entitled to."

"Oh, he definitely thinks he's entitled to me. Apparently, that was the price I paid when he gave me his name."

"Joanna's called me too."

I groaned.

"Jack filed the papers and she's upset about it."

"She'll get over it."

Claire paused. "Look, my Aunt Ruth still isn't cleared to be home by herself. She plans on staying with my parents at least another week, maybe two. Stay there. Let Blake and Joanna come to terms with your separation. Another week or two will be good for everyone."

"Do you think I'm running away?" I asked, suddenly feeling like a chicken for coming here to hide.

She made a sound. "No. I think your life turned upside down, and you're taking a timeout, a breather so you don't end up on one of those god-awful reality shows about desperate housewives."

I laughed. "I don't feel like I'm running away, you know? But it feels good to not have to live up to Blake and Joanna's standards."

"Your sister totally belongs in that movie *The Stepford Wives*."

I grinned. Claire was right.

"Take this time, Talie. When you get back, you'll be getting another job, getting a place of your own, and returning to the real world. Play hooky as long as you can. Being an adult isn't all it's cracked up to be."

Of their own accord, my eyes drifted toward the window and out at Gavin's house. My libido kicked up and the prospect of even just one more encounter with him was enough to make me want to stay.

"I guess someone needs to feed Salty." I reasoned.

"You two getting along better?"

I laughed. "Hell no. But Aunt Ruth would feel better if someone was here to look after him."

"Absolutely." I had no idea if she was agreeing because it was true or if she was just letting me convince myself to stay.

"Okay, tell Ruth I'll stay another week."

"I will. And Talie?"

"Hmm?"

"Next time I call, answer the damn phone."

14

Talie

It felt good to be able to stay here. In truth, I wasn't ready to go home. Being at the beach was relaxing, and despite everything going on in my life at home, I felt utterly at ease here.

With an extra spring in my step, I went to change out of my sand-ridden bathing suit. As soon as I turned on the bathroom light, I noticed I didn't do a very good job applying sunblock. My shoulders and back were very red. Thankfully, my face wasn't burned because when I wasn't wearing my hat, I was lying facedown, which kept most the sun off my face.

I took a cool shower, grimacing when the spray hit the sun-scorched area. I was going to be hurting later. The jellyfish sting on my lower arm and wrist was healing nicely. The rash wasn't nearly as red as before and the pain was gone. I'd been applying hydrocortisone cream to the area, and it was helping.

Once the sand was rinsed away and I felt refreshed, I climbed out and dried, slipping into a short, white cotton dress. It showed off my newly tanned limbs from spending so much time in the sun. I forwent a bra because I was afraid the straps would hurt my burn.

After combing a bit of mousse into my hair, I left it to air dry. The shorter length was so much easier and I hadn't realized my hair had natural body to it. All this time, I kept it too long, constantly blowing it out, fighting against the frizz, when really, if I'd left it alone, I might have realized the strands would dry into effortless waves.

Maybe the rest of my life was like that. Maybe I spent too long trying too hard, forcing things to be a certain way and never quite achieving happiness. Maybe if I'd taken a step back, I would have realized if my life was supposed to be that way, it wouldn't have been such a fight. It wouldn't have been so hard.

My stomach growled and I went into the kitchen and pulled a small packet of preformed hamburgers out of the fridge. I didn't cook much, but a grilled burger out on the deck sounded pretty darn good.

I laid the meat on the counter and went outside and uncovered a small grill that was stuffed back in the very corner of the deck. Judging from the looks of it, Aunt Ruth hardly ever used it. Thankfully, there was a gauge on the side of the propane tank signaling there was more than enough propane for grilling.

After setting aside the grill cover, I opened the tank and checked under the hood. The racks were blackened from use and the interior was small and slightly grimy.

The heat would loosen up the worst of the grime and then I could scrape it down before adding the burgers. I turned on the pilot light and closed the lid. Then I struck the igniter button and turned on all the valves, keeping them on high to blast the inside with sanitizing flames.

While that was burning, I rummaged in the kitchen until I found her grill brush. Back at the tank, I opened the lid only to frown. The thing never lit! "Stupid grill," I muttered, leaning down to make sure I did have the tank open and there was enough fuel.

Yes and yes. So I hit the igniter button again, listening to it catch. No flames. I smelled the propane, but for some reason it wasn't lighting. After a few more failed attempts, I growled and stomped into the kitchen to get the lighter I saw in a drawer. It was the kind with the long black nose. I remember as a kid we had an old grill and my dad would use his lighter and stick it up from the underside to light the flame.

Couldn't be that hard.

I left the grill lid open and bent under, looking for the little area to stick the lighter. When I found it, I turned on the gas and stuck it up inside. I stood to see if it was working when a great whoosh and blast of heat exploded right in front of me.

"Ahh!" I yelled and stumbled back as a huge burst of flames shot up from inside the grill. They raged with a ferocity I couldn't understand as I sat there on my butt on the floor of the deck, looking up at the growing yellow and red blaze.

I jumped to my feet and reached for the lid to close it and smother the flames. Only, the fire was much too high for me to reach the lid. I stood there in growing horror as the fire took on a life of its own. If I didn't do something fast, I was going to reduce poor Aunt Ruth's beach house to ash!

I tossed aside the lighter and ran into the house to look under the sink for a fire extinguisher. Of course there wasn't one. So I spent precious moments searching and coming up empty. In a last-ditch effort, I grabbed a box of baking powder and a couple bottles of water and prayed it would be enough.

The heat from the fire was intense and the sunburn on my skin felt tight as my body grew hot. The wind from the water was only feeding the flames, and I watched in horror as the grill's cover lying just below somehow caught and started to burn.

I opened a bottle of the water and dumped it on the cover. The flames extinguished a little, but it wasn't nearly enough to stop them completely.

I heard a shout behind me, but I was too busy freaking out to look. I ripped open the box of baking powder and started flinging it everywhere. It fell around me like heavy snow.

Some of the flames began to lessen and my forehead broke out in a grimy sweat.

A flash of movement from the other side of the flames caught my eye, and then the sound of a fire extinguisher depressing its foam-like material filled my ears. I watched as the white foamy spray smothered the insistent flames and coated everything around me and the grill.

When the fire was out, I breathed a sigh of relief and looked up.

Gavin was standing there in nothing but a pair of those tight boxer briefs, wielding the red can like he was some kind of badass.

"Are you trying to burn down the house!" he roared.

I threw up my hands. I so didn't need this right now. "Yes, that's exactly what I was trying to do!" I spat.

"What the hell were you doing?" he said, dropping the can at his feet. "What kind of idiot turns all the burners to high and then lights a grill?"

"Don't you talk to me like that!" I clutched the baking soda box and remaining bottle of water.

He stalked around the mess and grabbed at the bottle and box. "This is the best you could do?" he cracked. "Honey, you are a danger to yourself and this entire beach!"

His words hurt me. Made me feel stupid. "I didn't ask you to come running over here!" I roared, drawing myself up to my full height. "I can take care of myself!"

Gavin dumped the bottle and box onto the deck and grabbed me, yanking me roughly into his arms. His mouth descended immediately and something in the back of my head shouted, *Yes!* The kiss was rough and demanding. My hands rushed over his body, trying to take in everything it could feel. I gripped at his arms, hanging on for dear life, refusing to break the kiss.

Gavin reached around and palmed my butt, lifting me so my legs wrapped around his waist. I growled in the back of my throat when I felt the evidence of his arousal against my core. Without breaking the kiss, he stepped around the mess and carried me into the house.

As soon as the sliders were shut behind us, he slammed me up against the wall, using his body to pin me there as he reached down and lifted the hem of my dress. Both my hands were clutched in his hair, holding him tightly as my mouth explored his.

His skin was cool from being inside with the air-conditioning, and it felt like a breath of fresh air against my overheated frame. Once my dress was around my waist, he shoved his boxers down and thrust into me in one hard movement.

I cried out as he speared me with his unyielding rod. Goose bumps erupted over my entire body as he lifted me at the waist, moving me up and down along his shaft.

My nails clawed at the back of his shoulders, and I leaned forward and fastened my lips on the skin just beneath his neck. Little mewling sounds came out of me as he impaled me over and over again. I grew taut, strung tight, as my body begged for release.

Both Gavin's hands slapped the wall on either side of my head, and I tightened my thighs around him. My back slid up the wall as he surged into me, and a shout tore from his throat. God, the feeling of him quivering inside me was unlike anything I'd ever felt before.

I ground down on him, so close to release, but not quite there. Gavin sensed my desperation and reached between us, pinching my enlarged, throbbing clit, and I broke apart. My teeth sank into the flesh of his shoulder as I rode the wave of release.

I collapsed against his chest, my cheek lying flat against him as I gasped for precious breath. He chuckled and wrapped his strong arms around me, supporting all my weight.

I could still feel him inside me and I closed my eyes, trying to memorize the way he felt. I knew in just mere seconds he would pull away. He would likely act like nothing happened, like what we just did wasn't a big deal.

It wasn't.

Was it?

I think maybe it was.

I think maybe I wanted more.

Oh, hell. I didn't think. I knew I wanted more.

To my intense surprise, he didn't put me on my feet. He didn't pull out of me. Instead, he walked over to the couch and sat down, keeping us connected. I kept my cheek on his shoulder, not ready to look up into his eyes. I wasn't ready to confirm how little this meant to him, not after I admitted I wanted more.

His hand rubbed up my back and across the sunburn. I flinched. He stilled and I felt his head look down. He sighed heavily. "You got a sunburn?"

"It was an accident." I defended.

"You really are a disaster waiting to happen," he said. It was without heat, though, without malice. It almost sounded like it caused him regret. I started to lift my head to ask him what it meant when I heard him mutter, "I won't be around to watch."

He lifted me off him and sat me on the couch. In one quick movement, he yanked down my dress and covered up his privates.

The next sound I heard was the door closing quietly behind him.

15

Talie

Some jerk down the beach was teasing me with the scent of grilling meat. I mean, really. If it wasn't bad enough, I almost caught myself on fire, had amazing sex with a guy who confused the hell out of me and then left, but now I had to be out here on this filthy deck, scrubbing up baking soda and whatever the hell the stuff was from inside an extinguisher.

I was pretty sure I owed Aunt Ruth a new grill. This one was toast. Literally.

Maybe once I was done, I would drive into Surf City to Island Delights and get a giant chocolate malt and a burger that I didn't have to cook. "How was I supposed to know the interior of the grill would fill up with propane and then explode?" I muttered to myself.

Well, I sure as hell knew now.

As I cleaned, I kept my back turned to Gavin's place. I didn't need a reminder of our all-sex-nothing-else relationship. The satisfied ache between my legs was reminder enough. What did he mean by *I won't be around to watch?* He acted like I had some kind of death wish. It was an accident.

"All I wanted was a stupid hamburger," I muttered.

"Here," a deep voice said from close by.

My head snapped up as Gavin came strutting across the deck, wearing a pair of navy-blue gym shorts and carrying a white paper plate. I stood up, brushing off my hands and glancing down at my soot-streaked dress.

"What's this?"

"I was grilling out and figured I'd bring you a burger since, you know, you murdered that poor grill." The affection in his tone caught me off guard.

I took the plate and looked down at the perfectly grilled patty on a fluffy sesame seed bun. "Thank you."

"I got some sweet tea at my place if you're interested," he said, and I caught the flash of vulnerability in his eyes just before he turned and walked away.

I followed along behind him, so intrigued. Gavin was definitely a guy who kept his cards against his chest, and this was the first time he'd ever offered to spend any time with me beyond getting naked.

On his deck, he poured us both large glasses of sweet iced tea and then picked up a plate with two loaded burgers on it and swung his leg up over a nearby deck chair. I stood there holding a red solo cup and a paper plate, watching him, wondering what to do next.

He didn't look over when he patted the seat beside him, but kept his eyes trained out to sea. I sat down and placed my cup on the armrest and plate in my lap. I didn't realize how tired I was until I sat down. Too much sun followed by too much excitement turned me into an exhausted lady.

I watched the waves for long moments, staring off into the horizon and sipping the insanely sweet tea Gavin gave me. When I finally bit into the burger, I sighed in appreciation. It was so good.

Out of the corner of my eye, I saw him smile and then shove the remaining hunk of the first burger into his mouth.

"So how long have you lived here?" I asked around another bite.

The cup paused halfway to his lips. A muscle ticked in the side of his jaw. "Almost two years."

"Do you like it?" Was it just me or did the air around us turn a little bit cold? I knew he said he was a private man, but my question seemed innocent enough.

"I like the beach," he said, offering no other information.

Okay, so talking about him clearly was off-limits. Was I supposed to sit here and say nothing at all? If so, why did he invite me over?

Maybe if I told him how much of a wreck my life was, he wouldn't feel like his was so bad it had to be kept secret.

"So before I came here, I got fired from my job," I blurted.

He shook his head. "Did you set the place on fire?" He joked.

"I wouldn't sleep with my boss." I picked a couple seeds off the top of my burger while I spoke.

He made a choking sound and for the first time since I got here, he looked at me. His intense eyes met mine. "Are you serious?"

I nodded. "Well, sort of." I began. "I'm trained in medical billing and coding. I worked for a doctor and when he took over the practice, he hired all new staff but me. All the girls were gorgeous, well-endowed, and all too willing to *work* after hours."

"And you wouldn't," he said, his voice flat.

"No. So when one of the regulars at the practice came in and made a big stink over her bill, he took that as his opportunity to fire me for not being a team player."

"Fuck him."

"I think if I had, I would still have a job," I quipped.

He barked a laugh.

"Doctor's are egomaniacs," I said. "They think everyone should treat them like a god."

"They're just people like everyone else."

"Exactly." I agreed.

"So you got fired and came here?"

"Something like that." I wasn't about to tell him all of my business.

A few minutes of silence passed between us. "Do you have a job?"

"I used to," he replied, sitting back and propping his feet up on the railing of the deck.

It was really hard to have a conversation with someone who didn't want to participate.

"How long are you here for?" he asked.

"I was supposed to go home tomorrow, but I extended it for another week or so."

"Another week, huh?"

"Don't worry. I won't catch anything else on fire." I joked.

His smile flashed. He didn't smile very often or for very long, but I lived for those brief moments of happiness that visited his strong, unshaven jaw.

"Maybe we can hang out. You can teach me how to surf?" I suggested.

"No," he said roughly, keeping his gaze away from mine. "I don't make good company."

He wasn't lying about that. Even still, his rejection stung. All the times Blake told me no one else would want me replayed in the back of my mind like a bad song.

"Right." I stood from the chair and tossed my cup and plate into a nearby trash bag. "Well, thanks for the burger. And for coming over with an extinguisher. I'm going to have to buy one for Aunt Ruth before I leave."

He made a sound and didn't glance away from the view. The tension between my shoulder blades didn't ease until I stepped onto my own deck. I wasn't sure what just happened, but I did know it twisted up my stomach into uncomfortable knots. I decided right then and there that no matter how much longer I was on this island, I was going to do everything I could to stay the hell away from Gavin.

16

Talie

When you go to the beach, step onto the sand, and glance out over the vast expanse of sea, you think to yourself that nothing in the world is bigger. That nothing in the world can make you feel as small as you do in that moment.

And then the sun goes down.

The stars light up the onyx sky and glitter like the most flawless collection of diamonds ever found. Curled up in a blanket, sitting under that kind of sky while hearing nothing but the waves crashing against the darkened, empty shoreline...

That is when a person feels smallest.

And most at peace.

I gazed up at the never-ending sky as the wind off the water carried away my inner turmoil and brought a certain stillness within myself. A certain kind of truce. As if my broken heart and troubled thoughts declared for at least tonight they would let me be.

The wind was chilly, but I wasn't ready to go inside, so I pulled the chenille blanket around me just a little bit closer. My sunburn made me feel colder than I actually was. Tomorrow I was going to have to stay out of the sun and at the very least wear a shirt to cover the worst of it. Maybe I would go grocery shopping and rent a couple movies, make it a day in.

And of course my decision to stay inside had nothing to do with avoiding Gavin.

It was because of my sunburn.

Uh-huh.

I had enough guy problems to wallow in without adding his still-stinging rejection to the list.

Maybe staying here wasn't the best decision. Maybe I should pack up and go home, face my future head on and deal with my past.

And Blake was definitely in my past.

I was sorry that Claire had to bear the brunt of his anger, although from the sounds of it, he didn't show his slimy side to many. I was glad for it. Not to save my reputation, but just because my family didn't need to be subjected to my poor choice.

I was hiding. Delaying the inevitable. Who cared if Blake was pissed and would pitch a fit when I refused to come home? Who cared if Joanna would invite me to lunch and sit silently (and not so silently) judging me?

Suddenly, I felt so incredibly weary. Tired of trying to be who everyone else wanted to be. Trying to tell myself that if I just tried a little harder, my life would fall into place.

Movement off to the side caught my attention, and I sat up, turning in the direction of the stairs. A figure moved out of the darkness toward me. His blond hair was covered beneath a baseball hat and he was actually wearing a shirt, a white one that seemed to glow against the backdrop of night.

"Hey," he said, stepping closer.

"Hey," I replied, not sure what else to say. I was surprised to see him. I thought he wasn't good company.

"Can I sit?" He gestured toward the chair beside me.

"Sure."

He lowered himself in the chair, sitting forward with his elbows resting on his knees. I sat back, feeling like he obviously came here to say something so I would wait for him to say it.

"I'm an ass," he said, turning slightly so his words could be heard over the gusting wind.

"Ya think?"

I saw the flash of his white teeth. "I deserved that."

I certainly wasn't going to deny it. His moody, sexy behavior probably needed some kind of medication.

Gavin expelled a heavy sigh and then stood abruptly. He placed his hands on his hips and stared out into the darkness, keeping his back turned to me.

"I'm not available," he said.

Panic bloomed in my chest and a sick feeling spread throughout my body. "You said you lived alone."

Did he have a girlfriend? A wife? Was she maybe out of town? Had I done to some other woman what was just done to me? The thought made me physically ill. I knew how it felt to have someone you loved and trusted take advantage of you, to make you feel like you weren't enough. I couldn't do that to someone else. I couldn't.

"I do," he replied, swinging around to look at me.

I glanced up, the hammering of my heart making his words harder to hear.

He cocked his head to the side and looked at me. "I'm not involved with anyone."

"Oh..." I blew out a breath and the sick feeling began to ease. "Being the other woman is not on my lifelong to-do list."

"Yeah, and being a cheating, lying dickhead isn't on mine."

I guess that meant he was against cheating.

"Then...?" I asked, letting the question dangle in the breeze.

He leaned back against the railing and looked at me. "I'm not available emotionally. I live here for solitude, to be alone. I don't have room in my life for someone. I can't hang out. I can't talk about my life. I just... I can't."

The veiled pain behind his words caused my heart to constrict. What happened to him?

"But you can have sex?" I said. Gavin might have had a rough time, but he wasn't the only one. And he wasn't getting off the hook that easily.

"I'm a guy," he said, as if that explained everything.

I guess it sort of did. He had urges, needs. Wasn't it the same with me? Hadn't I been starving for human contact, for a body-ripping orgasm? I couldn't judge him for something I was guilty of as well.

"I'm not available either," I said. "Emotionally."

He nodded like he already figured that out. "I shouldn't have been a jerk to you."

"It's okay," I said, meaning it.

He studied me for long moments as a strong gust of wind came up off the sea. I shivered and tucked the blanket just a little bit closer. Gavin moved, crouching down in front of my chair, reaching out to grasp the ends of the blanket.

From this close, I could see the intensity of his eyes. I could see the vulnerability he felt from coming here… I also could see desire.

"I can't offer you anything," he whispered. "But I'm asking you for something."

"What?" His closeness was driving me wild. Want burned through my veins as I studied the way the T-shirt stretched over his broad shoulders. Need eclipsed my thoughts as his hand tightened around the blanket and carefully drew me a little bit closer.

"I want you. I want to spend the next week burying my dick inside your body. I want to hear those little sounds of pleasure that you make just before you surrender to orgasm. I want uninhibited access to you until you leave."

My breath caught in my throat. He was totally propositioning me for sex.

"I won't answer your questions about my life. I won't ask you anything about yours. We aren't going to date. Emotions will be left at the door. This is sex—raw, physical, real. I can't give you anything, but I will promise you it will be good."

My underwear dampened. Clearly, I wasn't offended by his no-strings-attached proposal. In fact, nothing sounded better. I didn't need complications in my life, but sex with him would be nothing but pure pleasure.

We stared at each other for several moments. The heat from his hands soaked through my blanket and warmed my skin. When I moved, he released me and sat back. I stood and let the blanket trail behind me as I went to the sliding doors on the house.

He watched me walk away without saying a word. Once I was inside, the glow of the nearby lamp spilling out across the deck floor, I turned. Our eyes collided.

I opened the door as wide as it would go and then I stepped back, silently giving him my answer. Gavin pushed off the railing and prowled toward me across the deck with slow, unhurried steps.

17

Talie

He was insatiable. We had sex three times after he came inside. Once on the floor, once against the wall, and once across the kitchen counter.

Aunt Ruth would likely be appalled.

I had never been so satisfied.

After that third time, he carried me to the couch, where we both collapsed, sweaty and exhausted, and at some point I fell asleep. I woke with the sun streaming through the doors, and Gavin was gone.

My body ached in places that it hadn't ached in years as I wandered into the bathroom for a long, hot shower. Languid wasn't quite the word I would use to describe how I felt. I was definitely relaxed, but I also hadn't felt better.

God, the things he did to my body were brilliant. He knew exactly where to touch, where to stroke, and when to go hard at me. Frankly, I was glad he wasn't here. I might be embarrassed over all the noise I made last night. I wouldn't be surprised if my voice was hoarse.

The hot spray of the shower was like heaven raining down. I stood beneath the falling water, letting it coat my body, letting it wash away the remnants of last night. It didn't make me sad because I knew he'd be back. I didn't know when, but I knew I hadn't seen the last of Gavin.

I couldn't stand the heat of the water against my sunburn for very long, so I backed out and adjusted the temperature. I washed my hair first, noticing the way the bubbles slid down over my body on their way to the drain. I was so aware of myself, of my body... of how every single thing felt.

It was as if Gavin somehow flipped a switch within me and every little thing I missed before was now felt tenfold.

I turned after rinsing away the suds and let the spray caress my face, giving a sigh of appreciation.

Cold air from the bathroom washed over my backside when the shower door opened. I spun, blinking the water from my lashes.

Gavin stood there completely naked, his blue eyes glittering. I gave him a small smile, surprised to see him again so soon. New tendrils of desire curled up from within, coating the insides of my body. Oh, I wanted him. I didn't think I would ever *not* want him.

But I was a little nervous if my body would be able to accept him. The folds of my vagina were tender and swollen from last night's sex marathon.

He didn't say anything but picked up the bar of soap and lathered his hands. I turned around, giving him my back, and the feel of his large, soapy palms sliding over my skin was heaven. He kneaded my muscles, working the tension out of them, truly giving me that languid feeling.

His hands worked downward, each palm gripping my butt as he gave it a squeeze.

"Fuck, I love your body," he murmured, nuzzling his lips against the side of my neck. I felt the tip of his tongue sweep over my skin to catch some of the water. "Your curves are perfect. It gives me something to hold on to when I drive myself inside you."

I shuddered. He was a talker. He liked to tell me what he was going to do to me and when. It was freaking erotic. He shifted, bending at the knees, and his hardness brushed against my backside. After stroking himself against me for a few blissful minutes, his hands went back to washing, down the backs of my legs and flirting with the insides of my thighs.

His brazen hands slid upward, cupping around my front, delving into the short, textured curls of my sex, and he slipped a single finger along my folds. He growled a little at the slick heat that was waiting for him and nipped at my shoulder with his teeth.

On up he continued until both his hands were full with my breasts, and he pulled me back against him, my back against his front as he caressed the full, swollen globes. One hand came up to roughly grab my chin, and he turned my head to the side so he could cover my lips with his.

Rivulets of water slid between us as we kissed, some of the water entering my mouth and some entering his. He hunched around me so the spray didn't get me in the eyes, but bounced off his shoulder, like he was my personal umbrella.

The next thing I knew, he was turning us so I was out of the spray and it cascaded over his back as he knelt down in front of me. "Open for me," he rasped.

I braced one of my feet on the edge of the tub and the other against the far wall.

He looked up at me with water drops in his lashes, framing out the concentrated cobalt of his eyes. Water rushed over his cheeks and traced his lips. His fingers parted my folds. "Are you sore?" he asked, taking in the swollen yet still ready flesh.

"A little," I admitted.

Gavin brought his mouth up and covered my clit. He was gentle, carefully licking and suckling at the entire area until my legs shook so badly I couldn't stand.

He released me to stand up, lifting me off my feet and laying me across the bottom of the shower. The spray turned slightly cooler, but it was only hitting against my feet. Gavin pushed my legs apart and lowered onto his knees between them. He looked like some kind of model with water slicing over his cut, tanned body.

His hair was wet, darker than normal, and hung over his forehead, dripping even more water into his face. He still hadn't shaved and drops of water clung to the stubble like it did his lashes.

He came back down to lick me again, and I made a slight sound of protest yet also of pleasure. He lifted his head, gazing up across my body.

"Tell me what you want."

"No." I refused.

He lifted his brows. "No?"

I shook my head. "I want you to know. I want you to give me exactly what I want without having to ask."

A secret smile curved his lips. He came over me, his wet, stiff cock sliding right against my slit.

I moaned.

"I don't want to hurt you."

I opened my eyes and looked up at him. I know I wasn't supposed to know about him, that who he was didn't factor into this. But these kinds of situations taught you a lot about a person.

He could have pounded into me. He could have claimed me roughly like he did before. But he didn't. He knew I was sore. Whether he wanted to admit it or not, he cared how I felt. At least physically.

"You won't," I whispered, reaching up to touch his face.

He closed his eyes, cutting of the blue that had truly become my favorite color, and slid into me oh so carefully.

This wasn't the like the other times. This wasn't fast and hard. Gavin took his time. Slipping in and out of me with ease. It didn't hurt at all. My body knew him now. It accepted him… It trusted him.

As he moved, I trailed my fingers over his body, fingered the cuts of his abs, and gripped the strong hips at his waist. I'd never felt like this before. I'd never felt so utterly caught up in someone. He was all I saw, all I wanted to see.

I didn't know him, not at all. But I felt him. It was like we connected on a completely different level, one that went beyond knowing each other's favorite color and what led us here.

I felt the familiar tightening of my lower abs, and I knew that release was near. It was almost sad. I would miss having him inside me.

I glanced up. He was watching me. His eyes were eating up my face like he'd never really looked at me before. Our eyes connected and held. Chemistry bound us together, emotion welled up, and I knew he could feel it swirling between us.

It was too strong to deny.

"I'm going to need you to come, sweetheart," he said, unable to look away. His neck strained as he held back his own release.

I sucked the water off my bottom lip and nodded. He surged a little bit deeper and rocked upward, his length scraping the inner wall of my vagina.

Pleasure bloomed, like a flower under the warm, nourishing rays of the sun. It spread out through my limbs, making me weak. I held his gaze, even after my vision had gone blurry. I wanted him to see the way he affected me, the way he made my body sing.

I felt his seed spill into me. I welcomed it. He shuddered his release as the shower water continued to pour over our bodies.

Neither of us moved, even when the water turned frigidly cold. I couldn't feel it anyway. The only thing I could feel was him.

Gavin shifted his weight and reached down, pushing the wet strands of hair off my face. Our eyes met once more and something passed between us. Something more than physical attraction.

I turned my face into his hand without thinking. He stroked my lips with the pad of his thumb. Lowering himself, he grazed the side of my mouth with his, tenderly brushing a kiss against my flesh.

I looked up at him and smiled.

The moment was shattered.

It was almost like I could see reality creeping up on him. The chains of whatever bound him yanked him away just as he was beginning to open up.

He swallowed thickly, panic crossing his features. He pushed up away from me, putting space between us.

Then he left me there in the bottom of the shower, cold spray raining down upon me.

18

Talie

Gavin came to me twice more during the next three days. Both times were in the middle of the night. He would enter my room in the dark of the night and slip between the sheets to bring his body flush against mine.

Both times I was asleep, and he would bring me awake slowly, using his mouth and hands. In the morning, I would wake and he wouldn't be there, leaving me to wonder if it had only been a dream.

I knew it wasn't for two reasons:

1. My inner thighs were sticky from his release and

2. Dreams couldn't be that good.

Both mornings I would sit out on the deck with a mug full of coffee and pretend to look at the view. But I wasn't seeing the view. I was reliving the way he made my body tingle; I was remembering the sound of his soft sighs in the dark.

I knew why he was showing up at night. It was because of the feelings. The feelings that kept

bubbling to the surface whenever he looked into my
eyes or entered my body. He thought coming when I
was asleep would change it. He thought the darkness
would make what lay between us harder to see.

It wasn't.

I could be blind and I would still see the way he
made me feel.

What started out as intense chemistry was slowly
morphing into more.

He was scared. So was I.

Blake hurt me. He hurt me more than I ever
even realized. He'd been hurting me long before I
caught him cheating. He hurt me when he acted like I
was less than him, like I was privileged to be selected
by him. He belittled me in ways I never saw until I
took a very large step back and really looked. I know
that Blake likely loved me, but I didn't like his version
of love.

But even though Blake wasn't good for me, I
loved him. That in itself was the scariest thing of all.
Because if Blake—a man I loved—had that much
power to hurt me, then Gavin... Well, Gavin had the
power to completely obliterate me.

What I felt for Blake was merely a tenth of what
I felt for him.

I wasn't even in love with Gavin. Not yet. But I
wasn't going to be able to stop my heart's fall. *I should
march over there and tell him the deal is off. I should tell him I
am done being his no-strings-attached tryst.*

I couldn't.

I craved him like an addict craved heroine. My
body longed for him like it should water. There was
something intoxicating about being in his presence.
It's like every little thing, right down to the way I

drew in a breath, was intensified when Gavin was near.

When this little affair was over... I was very scared of what would happen.

I heard the door to his deck slide open, and he stepped out. He was eating a pack of snack cakes and standing at the railing in his boxers, looking out over the ocean. His hair was sticking up from sleep. He didn't glance this way. I was sure he didn't know I was looking.

He was a beautiful man.

Beautifully broken.

Something shattered him. I didn't know what it was or when it happened, but I knew he was broken. He thought all of him was out of order, but I knew different. I saw the signs of life behind his eyes. I saw the glimpses of existence when he thought I didn't. Gavin might be broken, but some of him could be put back together.

He turned from the railing and looked in my direction. He stilled when he saw me watching. He shoved the rest of his snack cake in his mouth and gestured to me while he was chewing.

I left the blanket in my chair and wandered across the sand, wearing a little pair of sleep shorts and a tank top with no bra. He was standing at the top of the stairs waiting, and when I stepped onto the deck, he took my coffee from my hands and took a healthy drink out of the mug.

Something in my belly squirmed at the knowledge he was sharing my cup. Yeah, silly, I know. We'd had sex many times. We'd exchanged more than we ever could just by sharing a cup. But some things were just intimate that way.

"I'm out of coffee," he said, handing the cup back to me.

"Keep it," I replied. I was too busy daydreaming to drink it anyway.

He must have been in a daydreaming frame of mind as well because he took my hand and tugged me along with him toward a lounge chair. He sat and pulled me into his lap.

Gavin's arms folded around me, his hands clutching the mug in front of us. His scratchy chin rested on my bare shoulder. "Cold this morning," he said, his voice secret-soft.

My eyes fluttered closed and something in me splintered. If there was any hope of keeping my feelings safe from him, I couldn't sit here in his lap, being cuddled like he wanted to protect me from the wind.

But, oh my God, I couldn't move.

Being in his arms like this was absolute heaven. The area just below my ribs burned with emotion, buzzed with the wings of a thousand butterflies. It was like I waited my entire life to be wrapped up in someone like this and the moment had finally arrived.

Please, God, don't let this moment be fleeting.

I took a chance and relaxed into him, letting him support the majority of my weight. He tucked me closer against him, so close I could feel his warm breath fan out against my neck.

I shut my eyes, trying to memorize this feeling, planning to bank it away. This feeling was almost more intense than sex. It was wrapping its way around my heart and squeezing. I had to remember. I had to remember this feeling so when it was gone I would never forget.

One of his arms pulled back so he could drink more of the coffee. When he was finished, I felt him study me. "You okay?"

I turned to glance over my shoulder at him. He was so incredibly close. My heart puffed up just looking at him. I smiled and nodded. "Mm-hmm."

"Come here," he murmured, setting aside the mug and pulling me in. I rested my cheek against his bare shoulder and folded my knees up against my chest. He was so much bigger that when he wrapped his arms around me, I was totally surrounded.

His faint coconut scent swirled around me, and I took a deep breath, letting my eyes flutter closed.

"What am I gonna do with you, Talie?" he mused, almost as if he were talking to himself.

Love me.

The thought caught me off guard. My insides stilled even as the rest of the world kept moving. Did I want Gavin to love me?

Did I love him?

My heart started to hammer, pounding tenaciously in my chest. Love was out of the question. It wasn't possible. I couldn't end one relationship and then just give my heart to another.

"Talie?" Gavin asked, dipping his chin down to where my head rested. "What's wrong?"

He was picking up on my feelings. He could feel the change in the air. We were so connected by some kind of invisible chemistry that I couldn't even freak out without him knowing.

I sat up. Gavin wrapped a large palm around my upper arm, like he was my anchor in a choppy sea. I looked at him wide-eyed, trying to understand what the hell was happening inside me.

"Your eyes are the color of sea glass," he murmured. "A hazy green."

"Gavin…" I started. Words bubbled up inside me like a witch's brew, threatening to spill out between us. He tucked a strand of wayward blond hair behind my ear and waited for me to continue.

Somewhere off to the side, a phone rang.

He sighed. "I shouldn't have brought that thing out here."

"You have a phone?" I said, surprise in my tone.

He chuckled. "I'm not a complete hermit."

He stood, taking me with him and setting me in the chair alone. I watched the strong muscles in his back as he snagged the phone from the chair behind us. "Yeah?" he said in way of greeting.

"Hey, Stitch," he said, and a little of his carefree mood disappeared.

I peeked around the chair at him, watching as he paced the deck.

"Yeah, yeah, I know," he said, running a hand through his hair.

Pause.

"I told you I'm not ready," he burst quietly, turning away from me. Tension radiated from his body.

Another pause.

"When?" He blew out a breath and muttered a curse word. "Today!"

I don't know if the person on the other end of the line had time to reply or not because then he growled. "Why didn't you tell me this before?"

I heard a raised voice on the other end but couldn't make out what he was saying.

"Fine," Gavin snapped.

More talking.

"Yes, I'll be there." He paused again. "I don't know."

He spun, spearing me with a look. Whatever had just been happening between us, those soft little moments… they were gone.

"Yeah. See you then." He snapped the phone shut and opened the back door, tossing it inside.

"Who was that?" I asked.

"I told you I won't talk about my life," he snapped.

I surged up from my seat. "It was one question!" I yelled. "*You're* the one who called me over here. *You're* the one who pulled me into your lap. *You're* the one who made me feel something."

Gavin's eyes narrowed. "I told you not to feel anything."

Oh shit, I was going to cry.

"Don't bother coming over tonight," I said, lifting my chin. "The door will be locked."

I strode off the deck, racing across the sand and into my house. Salty was sitting on the floor by the door when I rushed in. I burst into tears the second the door shut.

"Stupid!" I told myself and flung across the couch, burying my head in a pillow. The sobs came even though I told them not to. Once one bubbled out, the rest followed. I lay there and cried until I ran out of tears.

I must have been pretty pathetic because Salty, the cat who hated me, jumped up beside me and started to purr.

"He told me not to feel anything, Salty," I told the cat.

"But I didn't listen."

19

Talie

I spent the rest of the day inside. Not long after I peeled myself off the couch to take a shower, thick, dark clouds rolled over the ocean and lightning and thunder cracked through the sky. I watched from the window as the water turned choppy and violent, and then rain started to plunge from the sky.

The storm fit my mood exactly, and I welcomed it, glad the sun wasn't mocking me with its brilliant, bright rays.

I knew better than this.

Fool me once, shame on you. Fool me twice, shame on me.

Blake fooled me, and I blamed him for it. But what just happened with Gavin, I blamed that on myself. He told me. He told me he wasn't available. He told me up front all he wanted was sex. I agreed. Hell, I thought I wasn't available either.

I guess my heart never got the memo.

"Stupid heart," I muttered.

Maybe I was just reeling. Maybe I didn't feel as strongly about Gavin as I suspected. Perhaps the hurt

and humiliation over what Blake had done sent me on
a rebound spree that ended in rejection.

Rejection wasn't good for a woman who was just
told she couldn't fulfill her own husband's needs.

Yes, that was it.

Instead of being in love with Gavin, I was just a
stupid idiot.

Well, didn't I feel better?

(I didn't really feel better).

I made microwave butter-drenched popcorn and
sat myself in front of the TV. Lifetime was playing a
marathon of movies about scumbag men and the
women who got caught in their web of deceit and
treachery. It seemed symbiotic of my life so I settled
in to watch. Salty even settled beside me, which at
first made me extremely nervous. I mean, the cat had
done nothing but practically threaten my life with his
eyes of death since I got here.

But then he curled up in a little fluffy ball and
closed his eyes. The softness of his fur was sort of
comforting against my leg. Maybe I liked cats after all.

The storm raged on as Salty and I (okay, mostly
me) ate popcorn and watched movies. A couple
times, my phone rang, but I ignored it. I didn't feel
like talking to anyone.

I was well into my third movie about a woman
who escaped from an abusive husband and cut off all
her hair and was hiding in another state. The no-good
husband found her and was stalking her door at her
new place. He was hiding in the closet in her
bedroom... Of course she came home in the dark (do
people never turn on their lights?), walked into her
bedroom, and took off her shirt (of course she would

get attacked in her bra), and her husband chose that minute to burst out of the closet.

I screamed.

The banging on her door was just too realistic.

Except the banging continued after she ran out of the room.

Salty perked up and was staring at the stairs that led down to the door. The banging wasn't on the TV; it was here. On my front door.

The only person it could be was Gavin, but I told him not to come. Besides, even if it was him, he would come up onto the deck. Claire? The knocking/banging continued as I slowly got up from the couch. On the way toward the stairs, I grabbed my cell. Maybe it was Claire. Or maybe Aunt Ruth was home.

I wandered down the stairs as I pressed the button to light up the screen on my phone. The knocking was still insistent. For some reason, the fact the person was so aggressive with their knocking made me extremely nervous.

My hands were clammy when I lifted the phone to call up my texts. I had several from Claire.

Talie, I need to talk to you!

Talie, answer your phone!

When you get home, I'm going to smack you!

Okay, I won't.

Please, Talie! Pick up.

Fine. Blake figured out where you are. He's on his way.

I jerked to a stop and stared at the white door with only a small window at the top. Blake was coming?

More insistent knocking.

"I know you're here, Talie! Open the damn door!"

Well, shit. As if this day wasn't peachy enough.

My cheating soon-to-be ex was here.

20

Talie

I thought about not opening the door. I didn't have to. But that seemed a little childish. He'd driven all this way. Maybe there was something he really needed to talk about. Maybe there was an emergency of some kind.

With a sigh, I unlocked the door and pulled it open.

Blake was standing there with rain on his shoulders and dampening his hair. The small overhang at the front door didn't offer much in the way of protection.

Gee, what a shame.

"About time you open the door!" he said, rushing inside the house. "I'm soaked."

I didn't offer to get him a towel. "Why are you here, Blake?"

He pulled off his coat and then looked at me. "What the hell did you do to your hair?"

"I cut it," I replied defiantly, reaching up to finger the short, wavy strands.

"You can get it fixed," he said, as if my opinion didn't matter at all.

Had he been like this our entire marriage? Surely not. I would have noticed. Right?

"I like it," I declared, holding my ground.

He glanced at me before going up the stairs. He didn't even reply. Did my words not even require a response?

I went up the stairs after him, noting how he was studying the house with his construction-based eye. I'm sure this place was too small for him, too outdated and too quaint. It was all the things I thought made it special.

Turns out all those fancy things he said we were going to have weren't that important to me after all. I'd rather have a man who loved me.

A man like Gavin.

I shoved away the thought.

"Nice view," he said.

"You didn't come here to talk about the view."

He spun and took in my appearance from head to foot. I was still in my pajamas. I put them back on after my shower. I still wasn't wearing a bra and I hadn't bothered with a drop of makeup since I got here.

"You've had your time to pout. Get your stuff so we can go home."

How dare he come here and talk to me like that! "Pout?" I snapped. "You think I came here to pout? I came here because I couldn't stand to look at your face."

"I know you got fired from your job, Talie."

"Yeah, well, maybe if I was a little more like your secretary, I would still have a job."

His eyes narrowed. "He fired you because you wouldn't sleep with him?"

"It wasn't the official reason, but yeah."

"That son of a bitch," he muttered. "Doesn't he know who my family is?"

I rolled my eyes. "Not everyone cares about who you are, Blake."

"He wanted to ruin my name. He wanted to start rumors."

"This wasn't about you. It had nothing to do with you."

"He was trying to sleep with my wife!"

I snorted. "Please. Like you care. You weren't sleeping with me anyway."

His face turned beet red. I rather enjoyed it. "Maybe we should go home." I began. "Maybe I will go and get my job back, keep up with the *family* name. You can have your piece on the side, and I can have mine."

He looked like a vein in his head might explode. "You little bitch. How dare you talk to me like that?"

My stomach knotted. He never called me curse words. "You made the rules, Blake. I'm just following them."

"You will *not* cheat on me."

"It sucks thinking you don't have what it takes to satisfy your spouse, doesn't it?"

He stormed across the room and grabbed me by the shoulders, giving me a little shake. His eyes were furious. I grew nervous. It was fun taunting him, but perhaps I pushed him just a little too far.

"Don't you ever say anything like that to me again." His fingers dug into the flesh on my arms, squeezing me until I wanted to cry out.

"You're hurting me," I said, looking him straight in the eye. "Let go," I growled.

He released me and stepped back.

"I'm tired of this, Talie," he said, turning his back on me. "People are starting to talk. People want to know why you no longer work at the doctor's office. People want to know where you are."

I shrugged a shoulder. "Tell them I'm out of town."

"You're hurting the business." He spun to look at me.

"How could me being out of town hurt your business?"

He glared at me with a tight jaw.

"Oh," I said, the truth dawning. "This is about your father. Does he know?"

"About my little indiscretion? Yes."

"And?" I asked, wanting to know what my father-in-law thought of his son treating a woman this way.

"And he told me to tell you to get over it and get your ass back home."

I gasped. "He did not."

"He did, Talie. He says that whatever happens in our bedroom needs to stay there. Our marriage is not a community matter. People shouldn't be talking about it."

"Well, maybe you shouldn't have made it a community matter when you invited a slut into my bed!" I yelled.

"I told you I was sorry," he ground out.

"Yes, and then you told me you would do it again, just more discreetly."

"My father won't turn the business over to me until you're home and we're happy pillars of the community. He wants a certain family image for the company."

"The baby," I whispered, laying a hand on my stomach, thinking of the baby that wasn't even there. I looked up at him. "You were only going to give me a baby because he told you to."

"What difference does it make if you get what you want?"

He made me sick. So incredibly sick. I couldn't believe I wasted years on him.

"Get out," I said, my voice hoarse. I didn't think he could hurt me anymore than he already did.

I was wrong.

"Get your things."

I looked at him like he was an alien with four heads. "I'm not going anywhere with you. We're over. I want a divorce."

"I won't give you one."

"You will." Anger rumbled up in me. An anger unlike anything I'd ever felt before.

He walked up to me, toe-to-toe, and looked down (he was taller than me too; everyone was.). There was a challenge in his eye that I had no problem meeting. "It's over," I said, low.

"I will not let you cost me everything I've worked half my life to build," he growled. He reached out and snatched my arm. "Now go pack. We're leaving."

I began to struggle in his hold. Just the mere touch of his hand made me want to vomit. My God, how could I have ever fallen in love with him? His grip tightened and a look of determination crossed his features.

"Let go."

"Not until you learn who the boss in this relationship is."

I barked a laugh. I couldn't help it. "It sure as hell ain't you."

I cried out when his nails bit into the flesh of my arm. "Don't make me force you."

I'd never heard that tone before. It scared me.

I gave one last violent yank of my arm and at the same time he shoved me away, toward the bedroom. The force of us both sent me flying sideways. I hit the back of a chair and bounced off, falling onto the floor with a hard thump.

I rolled onto my back and looked up just in time to see a large hand reach out and spin Blake from behind. Seconds later, Blake was sprawled across the floor beside me.

I looked up, wild-eyed, to see Gavin standing there with glittering angry eyes. Beside me, Blake moaned and sat up, his lip busted and bleeding, already swelling to twice its size.

"What the hell!" he said. It sounded more like *butt zee ell.*

"You better stay down," Gavin threatened. "Because if you get up, I'll do it again."

When Gavin reached for me, Blake flinched. He pulled me up onto my feet, his eyes softening with concern. "Are you okay?"

I nodded. "I'm fine. I lost my balance."

"He shoved you."

"Who the hell are you?" Blake shouted from the floor.

"He's the neighbor," I told him.

"The neighbor?" Gavin said, like it wasn't the right answer.

I realized then he was wearing a shirt. A nice one. It was a crisp white polo that hugged his shoulders perfectly. With the polo he wore a pair of navy khakis and a pair of suede shoes that didn't have laces. I glanced up to see his hair was actually combed and not hanging over his forehead. "You're wearing clothes," I said, shocked.

He chuckled.

On the floor, Blake began to stutter, "You've seen him without clothes!"

We ignored him.

"I had to be somewhere."

I started to ask where and then I remembered I wasn't allowed to ask questions. "Oh."

"Talie," he said, "I need to explain."

"Really?" Was he actually going to tell me something about himself? Just the prospect made me all fluttery inside.

"Yeah. I—"

Blake got to his feet, cutting off the conversation I really wanted to have.

"We were in the middle of something," he said to Gavin. "You should leave."

Gavin looked like he was going to punch him again, and while that might be fun, I wasn't in the mood to peel these two off each other. I placed a gentle, restraining hand on Gavin's arm, and Blake looked like he swallowed a watermelon.

"Blake was just leaving," I said.

"I was not."

"Blake," I said, irritated and weary, "I'm not coming back with you. I mean it."

Blake began to say something, but Gavin cut him off.

"You're going somewhere with him?" He looked between us. "Talie, who is this?"

Blake drew himself up haughtily. "I'm her husband."

21

Talie

It was Gavin's turn to look like he swallowed a watermelon. The shock on his face was palpable, and it physically hurt to watch an array of emotions cross through his eyes.

Blake's declaration hurt him.

I didn't want to hurt him.

I needed to speak to him alone. To explain. I turned to Blake and gave him the death stare I learned from Salty. "Get out."

Blake's eyes widened. "Are you involved with him?"

"No," I answered. "But even if I was, it wouldn't be your business."

"I'm your husband!" he shouted.

"Not anymore." I reminded him. I pushed by and rushed down the stairs, opening up the front door. It was still pouring rain outside and the water was splashing inside and getting the tiles by the door wet, but I didn't care.

"Get. Out."

Blake actually came down the stairs, giving me a look like I was a complete stranger. "I'll fight you on this."

I drew myself up to my entire height and looked him in the eye. "Go ahead. I won't give in. Do your worst. When I come back, I will tell everyone in town exactly who you are. By the time we're done, no one will hire you, much less your father."

He paled.

"When you get the divorce papers, sign them."

He stepped out into the rain and turned back. For one fleeting moment, I saw the Blake I fell in love with. The Blake I thought I married. But then he was gone.

I slammed the door in his face and threw the lock. Before going back upstairs, I leaned against the door, trying to catch my breath. It was an ugly scene with Blake. And if I were honest with myself, a scene like that was the reason I was hiding out here at the beach. But it was over. And I handled him. It felt good. And judging from the look on Blake's face, I was going to get my divorce after all.

I heard a sound upstairs and thought about Gavin. Handling him wasn't going to be so easy. I cared about him deeply, and this conversation was probably going to hurt.

At the top of the stairs, I stopped and glanced around the room. It was empty. I exhaled a shaky breath, realizing Gavin had left. Tears filled my eyes, and I put my head in my hands. I hoped he would at least let me explain.

I guess that told me everything I needed to know about the way he felt for me.

I wandered over to the couch, using the hem of my tank as a tissue, and flopped down. A sound off to the side had me whipping my head around. Gavin was coming out of the kitchen, a pack of snack cakes and a towel in his hand.

He stayed.

"You have snack cakes."

"They're your favorite," I said simply.

"Tell me he was lying," he prompted.

I couldn't tell him that. "I thought you said you wouldn't ask me any questions."

He sat down on the coffee table in front of me, looking at my arm where Blake grabbed me. His eyes turned dark and stormy just like the outside sky. "You're going to have a bruise."

"It's not important."

He lifted the towel. It was wrapped around a bag of ice. Gently, he held it up to the area that bore the marks of Blake's fingers.

I reached out to take the ice, to hold it in place. Our hands bumped. We exchanged a charged look. I glanced away.

"I need to know," he said, low.

"He's my husband."

Gavin jerked up from the table and moved away. The distance he put between us hurt far worse than the bruise on my arm ever could.

"You're married," he said, like it was dirty.

"It isn't like that," I said. "We're separated. We're getting a divorce."

"He sure as hell didn't seem to want one," he snapped.

"Well, he didn't seem to care when he was sleeping around." I said it without heat. I couldn't find it in me to be angry about it anymore. It was as if that final scene with Blake was all the closure I needed. Now when I thought of him and his secretary in bed, all I felt was sad.

"He cheated on you?" he said, his voice dangerously low.

"Yes. He did. And then he told me he was going to keep cheating on me and I would learn to live with it."

"So you thought you would cheat on him?" he said. "Even the score?"

"What?" I said, suddenly confused. "No."

"You didn't think you should mention to me that you were married?"

"You said no questions!" I burst, getting up from the couch.

There was no way in hell he was going to be angry at me for doing what he wanted.

"You're married!" he yelled.

He glanced at my left hand, at my ring finger, wondering if he somehow missed a sign.

"I took it off the day we signed the separation papers."

He looked away.

I took a step toward him. "It's over between Blake and me."

"I can't do this," he said suddenly, looking panicked. I reached for him. He pulled away.

"Do what?" I asked.

"This." He gestured between us. "I felt like shit all day. The things I said to you, the look on your face..." His voice trailed away. "You make me want things, Talie."

I swallowed. My chest felt tight and it was hard to breathe. "You make me want things too."

He shook his head. "I came here to try and—" His words died abruptly and he looked at me. "I can't."

"I know you're upset about Blake."

"You're damn right I am," he growled. "That scum had his hands on you. You lived with him. You shared his bed. You let him touch you."

He sounded completely disgusted.

"I never said I didn't have a life before I came here."

"And I never asked."

"What happened to you, Gavin?" I whispered.

"I shouldn't have come." He bolted for the sliders.

"Gavin."

He stopped in his tracks.

"I want you here," I said, the words ripping from somewhere in my soul. The vulnerability I felt in that moment seemed like it could swallow me whole.

"Go home, Talie," Gavin whispered. "Go back to your husband."

Nothing could have prepared me for those words. They hurt worse than I even imagined.

Long after he had gone, I stood there, unmoving, in that spot.

22

Talie

It rained the entire night. All night long I lay in bed, listening the comforting sounds of rain pitter-patter against the roof.

Only I wasn't comforted by the sound.

How strange life could be. How one moment you're living your life, have everything planned, and then something happens and everything changes. The things you thought were most important, the people you thought loved you most, it all turned out to be not at all what you wanted.

I came here to get away, to figure out where to go from here.

I never imagined I'd find Gavin, that in two weeks time I would fall irrevocably in love with him. It was ridiculous, wasn't it? To love someone who kept his entire being to himself. But I didn't care who he was, not really. I didn't care what turned him into the jaded man who holed up in a beach house and kept everyone at bay.

I loved him.

Him.

Not the man everyone else knew. Not the man who had secrets.

I loved the man who ate way too many snack cakes, who surfed every morning, and no matter how hard he tried to convince himself otherwise, the man who cared about other people's wellbeing.

The problem with Gavin was that he cared too much. Caring hurt.

I should know.

The timing sucked, but I didn't care. I wasn't going to waste another ounce of my life on something that didn't make me truly happy.

When dawn finally broke over the horizon, I gave up on sleep and climbed out of bed. I took a moment to slip on a pair of cut-off shorts and a loose gray T-shirt. After brushing my teeth, I looked out on the beach.

It was still storming.

But Gavin was out there.

He was dressed in a dark wetsuit and held his surfboard at his side. The waves were violent and rough, crashing against the shore with a booming ferocity. He couldn't possibly mean to surf them like that. What the hell was he thinking?

I rushed out onto the deck, yelling his name, but he didn't hear. The deafening sound of the waves drowned out my voice.

I ran across the deck, my shirt already plastered to my body from the rain, and down the wooden steps. The sand was cold beneath my feet and damp from all the rain. I called out to him again, but he was closer to shore now, ready to go in the water.

Sand kicked up, hitting me in the back of my calves as I ran down the beach. I couldn't let him do this. He could get hurt.

Or worse.

I caught up to him, ankle deep in the ocean. I yelled his name and he spun. Surprise flickered in his gaze, and I pushed at my saturated hair, trying to keep my vision clear.

"What the hell are you doing?" I yelled.

"Surfing!"

"You can't surf in this weather!" I grabbed his arm.

Gently he pulled it away. "Go inside, Talie."

"Not without you!"

"I'm not coming!"

The wind ripped at my clothes and hair, goose bumps rose all over my body from the cold, and waves crashed against my legs, saturating my shorts completely.

"Please, Gavin." I took his hand, pulling him around. "Please don't go out there. You could get hurt."

A muscle ticked in his jaw. "I'll be fine."

"I love you!" I blurted out.

Time stopped.

We stood there utterly frozen, shock registering on his face. A whole host of emotions played over his features. Awe, happiness... regret.

"I don't love you," he said as the salty spray splattered our bodies.

My heart shattered. I knew it would.

"Go home," he said, rainwater slipping over his face, cascading across his features. It reminded me of that time in the shower. The time when everything between us shifted.

But it wasn't enough. Not even the insane, supercharged chemistry between us could make him feel something for me.

I turned and fled the beach. I raced up the stairs and into the house. Water and sand trailed behind me, but I just didn't care. I pulled out my suitcase and started throwing all my things inside, dumping it all in one giant heap.

Salty sat in the corner of the room, just watching. Once I was completely packed, I put out extra bowls of food for the cat and an extra bowl of water. I felt sort of bad about leaving him here all alone. But I couldn't stay.

I needed to go home. I needed to make a life for myself. A life that didn't include Gavin.

Tears blurred my vision as I ran through the rain to my car. The guys at the shop fixed it and delivered it several days ago, but this was the first time I was starting the engine.

"If you don't work," I threatened the car, "I'm taking you to a scrapyard."

It started on the first try.

I threw the old beater into reverse and backed out of the driveway. I couldn't help but look over at Gavin's place, the last time I'd ever see it. I did a double take when I realized he was watching me from the small portion of the deck that wrapped around the side of his house. He stood there, still wearing that black wetsuit, while rain poured around him. His lips moved. He might have called my name.

I put the car in drive and drove away.

23

Talie

The wind howled around my Jetta, making it feel unsteady on the road. Rain splashed against the windshield, making everything look tear-streaked. Or maybe it wasn't the rain. Maybe everything looked that way because I was crying.

I should have known that a girl like me couldn't have a tryst and not get emotionally involved. I wasn't made that way. I was soft inside. I wish I wasn't.

"It's okay, Talie," I told myself as I turned onto the main road that would lead me to the bridge. "You'll be fine."

And I would be. I might not ever trust my heart to another man again, but that wasn't the end of the world. I could still have a full and happy life.

And the family I wanted? I could always adopt.

The roads were wet, and large puddles washed up against my car as I drove down the road. I pulled out my cell and hit a button for Claire.

She answered on the second ring. "Did he show up there?" she asked immediately.

"Oh yeah."

"And?"

"And I told him if he didn't give me a divorce, I'd ruin his family name."

She snorted. "He's going to do that all by himself."

"What do you mean?"

"I mean that assistant of his is talking. Running her mouth all over town that the reason you left was because he's leaving you for her."

I laughed. "She can have him."

"You okay?" Claire said, her voice turning serious.

"Not really," I answered as the bridge came into view. There were barely any cars on the road because of the storm. Most people had enough sense to stay inside until it passed.

"I'm sorry," she said. I knew she meant it.

My eyes filled with tears again and I blinked them away. "I'm on my way back."

"What? I thought you were staying."

"I'm not going to hide from my life."

"You weren't hiding, Tal. You were taking a breather."

"My breather only made things worse."

Claire knew me well, and the second I said that, she knew there was more going on than I revealed. "What's going on, Talie?"

"I'll tell you when I get to your place."

"Should you be driving? You seem off."

"I'm fine."

I felt her doubt come through the phone. "I'll see you later," I said. I couldn't get into this now. I needed a little bit of time to process.

"Be careful," she said before I hung up the phone.

I tossed the phone into the seat beside me as I drove onto the bridge. The view from the center was beautiful. Even in the pounding rain. The car pointed downward, going down toward the mainland as I left the island behind.

Like a movie, scenes of my time spent with Gavin played through my head. The intensity of his eyes when he looked at me just before climax. The way his hair fell over his forehead. The way he never wore a shirt and shoved entire snack cakes into his mouth. The way it felt to be wrapped up in his arms...

A great boom of thunder cracked just overhead and startled me. I jerked out of my daydream, the wheel following my sudden movement. I veered to the right sharply. My reflexes kicked in and pulled the steering wheel back to the left.

The back end of the Jetta fishtailed and fought for traction against the too-slippery road. My crappy tires didn't find what they needed so my car began to spin.

The car catapulted across the road, and nothing I could do seemed to right it. I gave up steering and hit the brakes. The car locked up but didn't stop; it kept sliding. Short white poles, connected with white chain, bordered the road, separating it from the grassy area that led to the sound.

My car hit one head on and flipped over it.

The last thing I remember feeling was the cold tendrils of ocean water rushing against my skin.

24

Talie

The sterile odor of rubbing alcohol burned my nostrils and I wrinkled my nose against it. Awareness slowly creeped in around me and everything was dark. Panic was like a shot of adrenaline as I wondered why I couldn't see.

And then I realized my eyes were closed.

Duh.

I blinked, taking in the stark-white walls, the TV hanging from the wall, and the ugly curtain hanging open around the bed. Ugh, I was in the hospital.

I thought back to the last thing I remembered, and a sharp pain pierced my skull. I made a sound, thinking the doctor could have at least given me an Advil.

"Talie?" a familiar voice said from beside me. I opened my eyes again as the person hovered over me anxiously.

"Hey, Claire…"

She made a sound of relief and then smacked my leg.

"Ow!" I said without heat. "What was that for?"

"That was for almost dying!" She smacked me again. "And that was for scaring me to death!"

"I almost died?" I focused on her face. It was pale with dark smudges beneath her eyes. Her hair was messier than usual, and her shirt was on inside out.

"What's wrong with your shirt?"

"I was in a hurry to get here." She sniffed.

"How long have I been out?"

"About twenty-four hours."

"And in those twenty-four hours you couldn't go in the bathroom and fix it?"

She made a strangled sound and flung herself on top of me. "Thank God you're okay!"

The breath hissed between my teeth. My entire body hurt. "My car," I said, the memory of the accident coming back in hazy flashes.

"Is totaled."

"I didn't like it anyway."

Claire laughed. "Me either."

"What's a girl gotta do to get some pain meds around here?"

Claire's smile fell away and concern filled her face. "I'll go get the doctor, tell him you're awake."

"Want me to just push the call button?"

"Nah, the doctor's hot."

I laughed. The action hurt my ribs and I groaned.

Claire rushed from the room, leaving me alone. I wondered how she found me, how she knew I was here. I wondered how long I lay on the side of the road before someone came by and called for help.

I wondered what Gavin was doing and if he was okay.

I shifted and a bandage slid onto my forehead. I pushed it back up, resting my head against the uncomfortable pillow on the bed.

I heard some commotion outside the door and I turned, listening to a few raised, muffled voices. Seconds later, the door swung open and someone rushed in. Gavin skidded to a halt, stopping near the end of the bed.

I felt my eyes widen as shock rippled through me. "Gavin," I rasped, pushing myself up to sit. My wrist ached and I slid a little, falling to the side. He came forward immediately, gently sliding his arm around my back and helping me right myself.

He looked awful. Red-rimmed eyes, wild hair, haggard cheeks, and wrinkled clothes. I was still trying to get used to him with clothes. Today's selection was low-riding jeans (first time I'd ever seen him in jeans) and a navy T-shirt.

"Hey," he said softly, adjusting the blankets around my waist. "How are you feeling?"

"I've been better."

He perched on the side of the bed, concern plain on his face. Even looking the way he did, he was still beautiful. My heart ached seeing him here, seeing him show concern over someone he didn't love.

He picked up my wrist and applied two fingers to the inside, as if he were feeling for a pulse. "Headache? Muscle aches? Nausea?"

"Uhh," I said, trying to keep up.

Another man walked into the room, this one wearing a doctor's coat and being followed by Claire. She gave me a look that said she wanted to know details as soon as we were alone.

"Gavin," the doctor said, "let me do my job."

"Her pulse is elevated," he said, looking up to stare into my eyes. "Pupils seem to be normal."

"Gavin," the doc said again, "you don't work here anymore."

Work here? Gavin used to work here? Was he a doctor?

"You don't think I know that?" Gavin said, getting up from the bed to stare at the doctor.

Claire was right. He was hot. He had very dark hair, practically black, and light, icy-blue eyes. His face was clean-shaven (unlike Gavin's) and his jaw was square.

"You should wait outside," hottie doctor said to Gavin.

"Stitch, you know I can't do that."

Stitch? Wasn't that who called him the other day when I was at his place? My head started to throb worse than before. My mind was swimming. I was so confused. What the hell was going on?

"You're not even supposed to be in here," Stitch said tightly.

"You know me," Gavin said, as if that made his trespassing okay.

You know me. I didn't realize how three small, insignificant words could hurt so much. The doctor knew Gavin? He knew him in ways I didn't, in ways that I likely never would.

"You aren't related to her, man. You have no connection. Wait outside."

Claire looked at me with big, round eyes. She was totally eating this up. Gavin made a sound in the back of his throat and turned toward the door, but he didn't go through. He tightened his fists at his sides like it was physically painful for him to leave.

"He can stay," I said, earning everyone's gaze.

Gavin turned back, relief written all over his exhausted face.

"Are you sure?" the doctor said.

I nodded.

Stitch sighed and approached my side. He performed a quick but thorough exam, checking my vitals and asking me a lot of the same questions that Gavin was firing off when he first bound into the room.

"You were very lucky," Stitch said, pulling back when he was done looking me over. "Some minor cuts and bruises, a sprained wrist, bruised ribs, and a hard knock on the head."

"Do you remember the accident?" Claire asked, coming up beside the doctor.

"The roads were slippery," I recalled. "I think I lost control of the car."

"It flipped over and rolled down the bank and landed partially in the sound," Gavin said from the other side of the room. His voice was dark and low.

"How did I get here?" I asked, looking at Claire.

She glanced over her shoulder at Gavin.

"I brought you in."

"You?" I said, shocked. Everyone looked at Gavin, waiting for him to offer more information. He didn't.

I looked at Claire. "How did you know I was here, then?"

"When you didn't show up at my place and your cell kept going straight to voicemail, I got worried. You didn't sound good last time we talked," she said, lowering her voice. "So I drove out here, went to Aunt Ruth's. He was there."

"Gavin?"

"I was getting you some clothes and stuff, checking on Salty," he muttered. "Your clothes weren't there."

"They were in the car with me."

He grunted.

Claire once again gave me a look that said I owed her a bunch of answers.

I sighed wearily. My whole body hurt. I glanced at Stitch. "I don't think the pain medicine you gave me is working."

Gavin stiffened and pushed away from the wall to come forward. "Are you in pain?"

"A little."

"I'd like to finish her exam alone," Stitch said, his voice leaving no room at all for negotiation.

"I'll be right outside," Claire said, letting herself out.

Gavin was slower to comply, but eventually he left, not saying if he was staying or not.

"Now that they're gone, do you mind telling me how you really feel?"

"Like hell."

He smiled. "Yeah, that sounds accurate."

"I'm really going to be okay?" I asked him. He was an easy guy to talk to. I didn't feel awkward around him at all. I wondered if that was because he knew Gavin.

"I don't see any reason not to be optimistic."

"Spoken like a true doctor."

"Hey, they don't hand out these white coats to just anyone."

I smiled.

"Ms. Ronson—" He began, but I cut him off.

"Talie," I said.

"Talie." He corrected. "Are you having any kind of cramping or discomfort in your abdominal area?"

I thought for a moment, really trying to concentrate on that part of my body. "No."

"That's good."

"Did the seatbelt do some damage to my waist?" I asked, lifting my hand to my belly.

"No," he said and paused.

"What is it!" I demanded.

"When you came in, we did a full workup of your blood, alcohol levels, etc."

I nodded, not understanding where he was going with this.

"Ms... Talie," he said. "You have low levels of HCG in your blood."

"HCG?"

He nodded. "We ran it again, just to be sure."

"What!" I said, beginning to panic.

"You're pregnant."

All the breath whooshed out of my lungs as disbelief took over. "Pregnant," I whispered after long moments.

"Because of the low levels of the hormone in your bloodstream, I would suspect you aren't very far along. I doubt a home pregnancy test would even give you a positive result."

I sat there in shock, barely hearing anything he said.

"Based on your surprise, I would guess that you weren't trying to get pregnant?"

"What?" I said, glancing up. "Uh, no. I wasn't trying."

"You asked about pain medicine. It's the reason you're feeling the majority of your injuries. I didn't give you anything for the pain yet."

"A baby…" I said, still trying to wrap my brain around the fact that I was pregnant.

"Now, we have certain medications that are safe for women in your condition, but I wanted—"

I gasped, cutting off whatever he was about to say. "Is the baby… is it okay?" Oh my God, the accident could have killed my baby.

Tears welled in my eyes.

"There is no reason at all to believe that there was any harm done to the fetus. Right now, it's very small and your body is designed to protect it."

Without thought, I placed my hand over my belly protectively. *My baby.*

"Now about the pain meds…" Stitch began.

"I don't want any," I said firmly. I wasn't about to do anything that might cause this little peanut any harm.

"We have some that are considered safe."

"No," I said. I would rather feel every ounce of pain than pump some drug into my system while my little one was trying to form.

"Okay. If you change your mind, just have the nurses page me."

"I won't, but thank you."

He got a tender look on his face. "I would say this was a welcome surprise?"

"Oh, yes."

He stepped away from the bed. "You're going to need to stay at least one more night. Then we'll talk about springing you."

"Okay," I said, still distracted by the news. It was so utterly surreal.

He stopped almost to the door. "He's the father, isn't he?"

I glanced up. He couldn't hide his entire grimace. He wasn't supposed to be asking me personal questions like that. But I understood immediately why. Gavin and Stitch were friends.

Gavin was the father of this baby.

I didn't think it was possible to love it so much so fast, but it was all-consuming.

A moment of panic pricked my chest. "Did you tell him?"

"No. Doctor-patient confidentiality. But I do hope that you tell him." He gave me a look suggesting he didn't want me to hurt Gavin.

"Of course I will," I responded.

Stitch's face softened. "I really think you're exactly what he needs."

Before I could ask why, he left the room.

I sat there in the quiet with the white walls surrounding me, rubbing a hand over my stomach. Where mine and Gavin's baby grew.

Stitch was wrong. This baby and I weren't what Gavin needed. I wasn't what he wanted. He made that perfectly clear.

25

Talie

Claire entered the room almost as soon as Stitch
left. I probably should have asked him what the
people here in the hospital called him because I
doubted it was Stitch.

"Everything okay?" she asked, coming to sit
beside the bed in a stiff-looking chair.

"Yeah," I replied, still half a million miles away.
For a fleeting moment, I wondered how I was
supposed to do this. How I was supposed to act like
everything was normal, like nothing extraordinary just
happened.

I was pregnant.

With Gavin's child.

Was it totally stalker-ish and creepy to be thrilled
I was going to have a little piece of him forever?

I'd only known about this baby for minutes. This
baby was barely two weeks old. Yet I loved it with
every fiber of my being.

In that moment, I was glad this baby wasn't Blake's. I didn't want him to taint something so perfect and wonderful.

"Earth to Talie," Claire said from beside me.

I glanced at her guilty. "Sorry."

"Should I call the doctor back in here?"

"No, I'm good."

"Are you sure?"

I grinned. "You just want an excuse to see him again."

She widened her eyes. "Did you see his butt?" She mouthed the words OH MY, and I laughed.

"Can't say that I looked."

"You were too busy making eyes at *Gavin*."

"I was totally not."

"All right. Spill," she said, sitting up. "Clearly there has been a whole lot going on here on this island beyond you and the cat in a fight of wills."

"Salty and I called a truce."

She lifted her eyebrow. "Was that before or after you got involved with Gavin?"

I pressed my lips together.

"Please..." She scoffed. "Don't act like it isn't true. The sparks between you two are off the charts."

"You noticed?" I said, surprised. I thought he and I were the only ones who could feel that.

"Uh, yeah. I think everyone in this hospital noticed."

I lifted my eyebrows in silent inquiry.

"By the time I got here, you were already admitted and stable. Gavin was at Aunt Ruth's place, ripping apart your room for your clothes. He was very upset that you seemed to pack everything up and take it with you."

"I don't know why he would be surprised," I muttered. "He told me to go home."

"When we got back to the hospital, all the nurses made it a point to get out of his way. When I asked for your room, they asked me if I was family. I told them I was your sister." She grinned.

"You are," I said simply. She was the sister of my heart.

"Anyway, the nurse looked like she was going to tell him to stay out of your room, and he about bit her head off." She leaned close, a look of concern crossing her features. "I think he might have anger issues, Talie. How well do you know him?"

If she only knew.

"The doctor... Stitch appeared and intervened, telling the nurse that he was the one who brought you in. After that, they seemed to back off." Claire finished.

"But he wasn't in here when I woke up."

"No, because some of your tests results came back and he was hounding Stitch for an update on your condition."

I had a moment of panic that maybe he knew about the baby already. Stitch said he didn't tell him, that he couldn't. It wasn't like I didn't want him to know. I was going to tell him. This was his baby too. But I wanted to be the one to tell him. I wanted to witness his initial reaction because that was the one that would tell me if he truly wanted to be a part of this child's life or not.

"But he was in here before that?"

"He didn't leave your side. Every time you so much as breathed heavily, he was up and checking all the monitors and IV."

Why would he do that? Why would he tell me he didn't love me, tell me to go home, and then come take up vigil at my bedside?

"What's going on between you two?" Claire asked. "Are you sleeping with him?"

I felt my face flush because, oh yes, I was sleeping with him, and oh yes, it was the best sex of my entire life.

Gavin entered, looking just as haggard and wrinkled as before. His blue eyes found me and held, skimming over my body like he was making sure I was okay.

I glanced at Claire. "Would you give us a while?"
She lifted her eyebrow.
"Please."
"Of course. I'll just go down to the cafeteria."
"Actually, why don't you go check on Salty?" I hated thinking of him being alone.

She looked at me like I lost my mind. "Did they get my purse out of the car?" I asked her.
"Yeah, it's over there."
"Would you please grab me some clothes somewhere? One of the surf shops or something? Unless of course they got my suitcase out of the wreckage too?" I glanced at Gavin since he was the one at the scene with me.

He shook his head. "That part was already underwater when I got you out."

Oh. Would I have sunk to the bottom of the sound if he hadn't showed up when he did? The thought made me shudder.

Gavin strode across the room to a small closet-looking cabinet and pulled out a white no-nonsense blanket and brought it over to me, draping it around my body.

The gesture melted my heart.

"There is cash in my purse," I told Claire.

She went to the door, bypassing my purse. "You can just pay me back later," she called.

"I'll be back later. I'll bring you some real food."

"Thanks, Claire."

When she was gone, Gavin said, "She's not really your sister, is she?"

"My best friend."

"What the hell were doing out driving, Talie? The weather was awful."

"What were you doing out surfing?" I countered.

He scowled. "That's different."

"Why?"

"Because I didn't almost die!" he shot out.

His little outburst rendered me momentarily speechless. It also hurt my already pounding head.

Before I could respond, he was moving, coming forward to sweep both arms around me and pull me up against his chest.

He was so warm and he smelled just like he always did. I buried my face in his neck as his hand pressed the back of my head even closer against him. Tears sprang to my eyes, but I refused to let them fall.

"When I saw your car flip and then disappear over the side of the road, I swear to God my heart almost stopped beating," he murmured, clutching me against him.

"You saw?" I replied, my words trapped against his chest.

I didn't think he heard me. He held me for long moments and then gently pulled me back to cover my mouth with his. The kiss wasn't like the ones we shared in the past. There was nothing urgent and hot about this kiss. There was nothing insistent and wild.

But it wielded more power than all the other ones combined.

He brushed his lips over me, and I felt it right down to my very soul. There was something utterly tender about the way he caressed my lips with his, like they were something fragile and he was deathly afraid I might shatter. His hand cupped the back of my head, supporting my weight, and his other arm slid around the small of my back, lifting me off the bed and against his firm body. When at last his tongue dipped into my mouth, it was like he was tasting me for the first time. He groaned at the slight contact and licked a little bit deeper, tangling us together in the most delicious way.

He took his time, kissing me how he never had before. With more emotion than he ever gave. Usually there was a part of him he always held back, but right now, as our mouths moved as one, I felt like I was finally getting to experience all of him.

And damn, it was devastating.

When he finally broke the kiss, he lifted his head just a fraction of an inch above mine and then came back for a soft, quick graze in the center of my mouth.

His eyes opened, and I struggled to focus on him because everything in my world was suddenly hazy.

"Did I hurt you, sweetheart?" he asked, swiping at a rogue tear with the pad of his thumb.

I shook my head no.

How was I supposed to be kissed like that—by him—and not cry?

"Did Stitch give you some pain meds?"

"No," I rasped as he pulled away.

He looked at me sharply. "No?"

"I told him I didn't want any. I wanted to stay clearheaded."

He frowned. "You're going to be even more sore tomorrow. I'll tell him you changed your mind."

I didn't argue. He could tell Stitch what he wanted, but I wasn't taking any meds. Yeah, now would have been a good time to tell him about the baby, but I wasn't ready yet. We had things to discuss first.

"You saw my accident?"

He pulled away slowly and snagged the chair with his foot, dragging it right up beside the bed. Once he was sitting in it, he leaned forward, running a hand through his already wild hair.

"I didn't see all of it, just the car flipping and disappearing from sight. I didn't see it roll." He paled a little as he spoke.

"How?"

"I followed you."

"Why would you follow me? You told me to leave."

"I told you to go home, Talie. To the beach house. I didn't mean for you to leave town."

"The beach house isn't my home, Gavin."

"Yeah," he said, looking away. "I know."

I started picking at the little white pill-balls on the blanket.

"I shouldn't have said what I did." Gavin began, his voice filling with regret. "I knew it would hurt you. When you went running through the storm back up the beach, I called to you, but you didn't hear."

He knew it would hurt me, yet he said it anyway.

"So I followed you. When I saw you driving away, I panicked. I was worried so I followed. I caught up just in time to see your car flip off the road."

"You said it rolled over the bank?"

His eyes seemed focus on the memory of what he saw. "I pulled up to the side of the road and jumped out of my car, leaving the engine running. Your car was upside down, only partially lying on the bank. With the current and the wind the way it was, I knew it was only a matter of time before the entire thing sank." As he spoke, his hand slid across the bed and intertwined with mine.

"I screamed your name, and when you didn't answer..." He looked up at me. "I was fucking scared."

"Gavin." I sighed. I reached up with my free hand and touched the side of his face. He leaned into the touch.

"I rushed up to the car and looked inside. Shit was everywhere and water... water was filling it up fast. If it hadn't been for the seatbelt—" He broke off, looking back up at me. "I pulled you out, talking to you, trying to get you to say something. But you were unconscious. I assessed your injuries as best I could and decided not to call an ambulance. I didn't want to risk waiting for them to arrive."

"You brought me to the hospital?"

He nodded. "They know me here," he said. "I pretty much took over the ER when I brought you in." He gave me a wry smile.

I couldn't help but return it.

But his smile didn't last very long. It faded then like a pair of blue jeans washed one too many times. "You were so still and pale," he whispered. "It was just like…"

He stopped talking and looked away.

"Just like what?"

When he didn't reply, I pressed. He was talking more to me right now than he ever had before, and I wanted to keep the conversation going.

Softly, I pushed my hands into the spiky hair at his forehead and wrapped my fingers around it, lifting his head so I could look in his eyes.

"Just like what, Gavin?"

Something in his expression twisted. He took a shuddering breath.

And then he replied.

"Just like the night my wife died."

26

Talie

He had a wife.

Gavin was married.

A woman who died.

She left him all alone.

"You were married?"

He tried to nod, but I was still gripping his hair. I released it, smoothing it back away from his face. It didn't stay down, but sprang right back up into crazy pieces.

"Tell me," I said softly, wanting nothing more than to listen.

He shook his head and looked away. The pain he was feeling was palpable. It lay heavy in the air. Now I understood that look I sometimes saw in his eyes, the look of someone with scars inside them.

I didn't push him any further. I didn't tell him I was sorry or coo little words to try and make him feel better. My words wouldn't help him. No one's words would. This was something he was going to have to live with every single day for the rest of his life.

Telling him I was sorry wouldn't even come close to easing that kind of pain.

We sat there in the room with nothing but the monitor beeping steadily behind us. I ran my fingers through his sun-kissed hair. The way it felt sliding between my fingers somehow eased the tightness in my chest.

"We were high school sweethearts," he said after a while. I continued stroking his hair, just letting him know I was there and I heard him.

"I knew I was going to marry her from the time I was sixteen years old. She was something," he said. The fondness in his voice made my eyes briefly close. "She hated math and loved Doritos. She was on the track team, the cross country the school had. She had these long legs that just went on for miles. They ate up the pavement with ease."

"What was her name?" I whispered.

"Danielle."

"It's a beautiful name."

He made a sound. "She hated it. Made everyone call her Dani."

He glanced up at me, his blue eyes full of memories. "She was a tomboy."

I smiled.

"Anyway, we went to college together. She graduated before me and got a job as a teacher and coach of a track team. When she graduated, I asked her to marry me. She said the only reason I wanted to marry her was so she could take care of me while I suffered through my residency at the hospital." He laughed. "But she said yes anyway, saying someone had to look after me."

Oh my God, my heart was tearing. Literally ripping in half for him. I didn't know how to feel this kind of pain. I didn't know how to help him, to make him feel better.

"You're a doctor?" I asked, trying to hide the catch in my voice.

"I went to med school. I have the degree. I never finished my residency, though. She died right after I started."

"Oh, Gavin." I sighed, once again pulling my fingers through his hair.

"That day, the day she died, sometimes it replays in the back of my mind... tormenting me. Reminding me that I let her down."

"How did you let her down?"

I wasn't sure if he heard me or if he just needed to say it all in his way.

"I'll never forget that day," he said, looking off into space. I might have thought he was no longer present in the room with me because of the faraway look in his eyes, but his hand reached out and his thick fingers wrapped around mine.

It was my turn to be his anchor.

And when Gavin began to talk, it was if I were right there in that day with him...

27

Gavin

The shifts at the hospital were going to kill me. I suddenly understood why half the doctors in the place were gray haired or bald. Dealing with life—with other people's lives—was demanding and draining. I couldn't afford to have a tired day. I couldn't afford to be low on energy. People depended on me. They looked to me for answers. Some of them looked to me for hope.

I never thought about that side of being a doctor. Being a doctor was always biology and chemistry, formulas and equations. My job was to look at a disease, a mutation trying to take up residence in someone's body, and come up with a way to get it out. To defeat it.

I never thought about the actual people these diseases were living in. I never thought about the human eyes that I would have to look into while they asked me if they were going to die.

How did a man do it? When their scientific equation, their scientific solution failed, then what? My failure could cost lives.

When I stepped into the apartment, the aroma of rich tomato sauce wafted through the air. God, I was starving. I couldn't remember the last time I ate something that wasn't from a vending machine. The day before yesterday maybe?

I stepped around the corner and she was there. I didn't need to drink coffee. If I wanted a boost of energy, all I had to do was look at her.

"Hey, handsome," Dani said, turning from the stove. Her caramel-colored hair fell down her back in a thick braid. "I'm making spaghetti."

She was dressed in a pair of black yoga pants and a loose T-shirt. She was beautiful to me. My hands itched to touch her and my feet obeyed, suddenly forgetting they were tired and taking me over so I could wrap my arms around her from behind and nuzzle her neck, playing at her collarbone with my tongue.

"Mmm," she said as I pulled her earlobe between my lips.

She spun in my hold, reaching up to kiss me, the kind of kiss that melted away days of being at the hospital. "How was school today?" I asked, pulling back but keeping her in my arms.

"Good. Track meet this Friday…"

I kissed her again, just because I could.

"The pasta is going to boil over!" She laughed, trying to push me away. Her attempt was pathetic because she liked when I was close.

"I have a noodle for you," I said, wagging my eyebrows at her.

"You did not just say that." She groaned, rolling her eyes.

I released her and she went to check the pasta, but before she could go, I pulled her back. "I love you."

"I love you, too." She swatted me with a kitchen towel. "Now go wash your hands."

After dinner, it was my turn to do the dishes. I tossed them in the sink and poured water over them, then turned away. "Let's go out for ice cream."

"How can you even think about food? I am stuffed."

"You know me." I joked. "I'm insatiable."

"One of the many things I love about you."

I winked.

"What about the dishes," she asked, lifting an eyebrow.

"They need to soak."

She giggled. "Fine. Let's go."

It was after eight, but the traffic on the roads was moderate. Jacksonville, North Carolina, was a place that never seemed to sleep completely. Yes, the roads slowed down, but because it was such a military town with young Marines and bars everywhere, the place never truly slept.

Cold Stone closed at nine, but I wasn't in a hurry because I knew we'd make it in time. It was a warm night, typical of the south, and we drove with the windows down. Dani had her bare feet propped up on the dash, singing along horribly to a country song on the radio. I couldn't help but glance at her as I drove. Long wisps of hair escaped her braid and fluttered around her head like a halo.

Maybe I should have realized that was my sign.

My sign that everything was about to change.

I should have known such an angel wouldn't be allowed to stay on Earth.

The car came out of nowhere. Running through the intersection, completely ignoring the red light. I saw it at the last second, reaching out and slamming my arm against her, trying to protect her even as I spun the wheel, trying to get out of the way of the speeding car.

But we didn't make it.

The sound of shattering glass and groaning metal weren't even loud enough to cover up her screams. I would hear those screams until I died.

When the car finally stopped, screeching to a halt on the side of the tree-lined boulevard, the sound of silence, the feeling of stillness washed over me.

In those few heartbeats, I knew everything was about to change.

"Dani!" I yelled, grappling with the seat belt, trying to get free. Her non-responsive behavior scared me, and I began to struggle harder.

Finally, it let me free and I dropped onto my side, ignoring the cutting glass and shouts from people running to help. I saw her lying in the seat beside me, hunched over with a single rivulet of blood running down her temple.

"Dani, baby," I said, reaching for her, wrapping my hand around her arm.

Behind me someone opened the driver's side door. "Are you okay?" someone yelled.

"Call 9-1-1!" I screamed.

The door on Dani's side was wrenched free. Hands appeared and lifted her out. I scrambled through the wreckage to free myself and drop beside her on the pavement. The scent of burning rubber and spilled gasoline filled the air. The sound of people talking, of people crying, pressed in around us. The distant sound of sirens headed in our direction was like a beacon of hope on a hopeless night.

"Dani," I said, "open your eyes."

In the dark, her lashes fluttered. Brown eyes looked up, unfocused and confused.

"Hey," I smiled. Relief like no other poured through my body, making my hands tremble. "Hey, babe. Thank God."

"Gavin?" she asked, her voice weak.

"Shh," I told her, brushing away the hair from her face. "There was an accident. Help is on its way."

Then I remembered I was a doctor. I could help her now.

I clicked into clinic mode, assessing her injuries, feeling for a pulse. She was hurt, hurt badly. It seemed like she had some internal bleeding and her breathing didn't sound right. I was afraid she had a punctured lung.

"Where's the ambulance!" I yelled over my shoulder.

No one offered me an answer.

It was dark out here, so dark. How was I supposed to make a diagnosis in the dark with no medical supplies, not even so much as a napkin to wipe her blood?

I palmed her cheek and gently turned her head in my direction. "Listen to me, Dani. Help is coming. Everything is going to be okay."

She smiled at the sound of my voice. But she didn't open her eyes.

"Stay with me, baby. I love you."

"I love you, too," she whispered.

And then she died.

That was the last smile I would ever see on her face. The last words I would ever hear her speak. She died there on the pavement on the side of the road littered with debris and strangers. The ambulance pulled up minutes after she died. Too late.

Too fucking late.

28

Talie

My face was wet with tears. My hand had long ago fallen away from his hair and into my lap. Gavin still held my other hand, never once breaking contact the entire time he spoke.

What he'd been through was horrible. Something no one should ever have to live. To watch the person you loved most in this world die on the side of a road while you stood by helpless was cruel.

I understood why he said he was emotionally unavailable. I understood all those times he pushed me away. All those times when I thought we were getting closer, when he was letting me in only to have a door slam closed.

He lost the only woman he'd ever loved. A woman who was supposed to be by his side forever. She didn't cheat on him or lie. She didn't wake up one day and decide he wasn't who she wanted. She was taken from him. Stolen by the worst kind of death.

And since that day, his life had been at a standstill. His life had never been the same.

What did you say when someone told you the story of how they were robbed of forever? What did you say when the man you loved sat broken and sorrowful right in front of you?

There wasn't anything I could ever say.

Gently, I tugged my hand free of his and carefully slid over, turning on my side to face him. Gavin lifted his head, his bloodshot eyes watching me. I lifted the covers of the little hospital bed, inviting him closer.

He didn't even hesitate. He stood and kicked off his shoes and slid right in next to me. The bed was small and he took up most the space, but I didn't care. When he held out his arm, I settled against him, laying my cheek on his chest.

I could hear the beat of his heart, the steady rhythm just below his ribs.

I tucked my arm around him, ignoring all the protests of my body. Everything that I had been through this last month seemed like nothing compared to what he'd survived.

We lay there a long time, neither of us uttering a word. Just being close to him was comfort enough. I said a prayer while I lay there. I said a prayer for Dani, that she found peace in the afterlife. And I said a prayer for Gavin, that somehow, someway he would eventually find peace too.

"Gavin?" I said after a while.

"Hmm?" He turned his head toward me. His lips brushed my forehead.

"What happened next?"

"I quit my residency. I didn't think I deserved to be a doctor anymore. I wasn't sure it was for me."

"But why?"

"I couldn't save her. When the going got tough and I was in that situation that had to be acted upon, I failed. I failed to save the life of my own wife. I let her down. I let her die."

Such guilt to carry around. Such a heavy weight.

"You did everything you could," I said, propping my chin on my hand and looking up at him.

"It wasn't enough."

I wasn't going to argue with him, not about this, not about something that clearly caused him so much pain.

But for the record, he was wrong.

"Then what happened?"

"I got a big settlement from the driver's insurance. I tried to turn it down. They sent it anyway. I don't know why they thought I would want that blood money. It felt wrong to take it. Like I was somehow benefiting from her death."

"What did you do?"

"I bought the beach house on Topsail and gave the rest to charity."

"And you've been there ever since."

"Yeah."

"How long have you been there, Gavin?" *How long have you been grieving alone?*

"Almost two years."

"She wasn't the only one who died in that accident. You died too," I said.

"Why did I get to live instead of her?" he whispered, agony in his tone.

"I don't know," I replied, honestly. "But I honestly think there was a reason. There is a reason for everything." I thought of the baby that I carried inside me. His reason for living... He had to live so he had something to leave behind.

"It should have been me."

"Dani wouldn't want you to carry around this much pain and guilt."

He shifted, wrapping me in both his arms. His hold was strong, and it hurt just a little, but I didn't say a word. Minutes later, I felt his lips on my forehead, pressing a gentle kiss to my hairline.

"Gavin?" I whispered.

"Yeah?" he whispered back.

"You saved me. You pulled me out of the car and you saved me."

"I couldn't watch you die on the side of the road."

That's why he drove me here himself. It's why he sat vigil beside my bed. He had to make sure I didn't die. He had to make sure he wasn't responsible for another death.

How horrible it must have been for him watching my car veer off the road. But he was still here. He hadn't run away.

"You know I'm going to be okay."

"I know."

"You don't have to stay here," I pressed. I didn't want him to leave, but I wasn't his obligation. "I know this must be hard for you. You can go home."

"I can't go home."

Probably not. My accident was too sharp of a reminder of what happened to Dani. Going home to an empty house would likely cause him to overthink. He couldn't be alone right now. I understood that.

"Well, you are a lot warmer than these pathetic rags they call blankets," I said, unable to stop myself from snuggling just a little bit closer.

His chuckle was warm and genuine. It fused together a little bit of the fracture that opened in my chest when he told me about his past. "Glad I can be of service."

"Claire thinks Stitch is totally hot," I said, trying to keep things light.

He laughed. "Her and every other woman in the South."

"I prefer blonds." The words slipped right out before I could snatch them back. The last thing I wanted to do was say something that would make him push me away again.

"Be sure and tell him that," Gavin replied, not bothered by the comment at all. "Maybe it will deflate some of his big head."

"Have you known him a long time?" Just from the fondness in his tone, I knew they were friends.

"We went to med school together." He cleared his throat. "He was here the night Dani was brought into the morgue."

I was glad at least someone had been here for him that night.

"He was the one who called that day, on my deck."

"Really?" I said, remembering the name, but not bothering to say so.

"The hospital has been holding a spot for me to come back, to finish up my residency. They're getting tired of waiting. I had a meeting here that day so we could talk about."

I remembered the way he was dressed the day he walked in on Blake and me. He likely just arrived home from the meeting. "Are you coming back to work?"

"I don't know," he said, his voice drifting far away again.

In that moment, I felt like I was holding on to a long string... and he was the kite attached to the end of it. Sometimes the wind wouldn't blow that heavily, and I was able to reel him in. Get him close. But then the wind would pick up and start pulling at the corners of the kite and lift it back up into the sky so it floated farther and farther away.

"You know a doctor should know better than to live off snack cakes." I teased.

He made a rude sound. "Nothing comes between a man and his snack cakes."

I smiled, but it quickly turned into a yawn.

"You should get some rest, sweetheart." Damn if he didn't punctuate those words by pressing his lips against my hairline.

I didn't want to go to sleep. I wanted to stay in this moment with him. I knew he might not be here when I woke up.

But he was too warm and too comfortable. My eyes began closing, taking longer and longer to reopen. I tried to tell myself to fight it, to stay awake. In this moment, the wind had died down. He was close. So close.

My last thought before I succumbed to slumber was to wonder how long until the wind started to blowing again, how long until he was yanked back into the sky.

29

Talie

I was alone when I woke the next morning.

I suspected I would be, but that didn't stop the little pang of sadness when I reached for him and he wasn't there.

I hoped things weren't as bleak for him in this new day. I hoped that telling someone about what happened to Dani helped him heal, if only a little.

There was no clock on the table beside the bed, and the curtain was partially pulled around, concealing the wall clock, so I pushed up and leaned forward to get a peek at the time.

My movement was cut short when pain stopped me in my tracks. I was so sore. Even more so than yesterday. They told me I would be, that it was part of the healing process. The healing process sucked.

It made me think longingly of pain medicine.

And then I remembered.

I remembered I was pregnant.

A smile curved my lips and I put a hand to my belly. "Hey, peanut," I whispered and stretched my

arms and legs slightly, trying to work out the soreness.
I needed to move around. Lying in this bed was only
making it worse.

I swung my legs over the side of the bed and
used the IV stand as support to stand up. My feet
were bare and the tile floor was cold. I was dressed in
one of those stupid, too-large hospital gowns and it
hung down past my knees.

My entire body felt like a giant bruise, but I kept
moving. After maneuvering the IV stand, I used the
facilities and washed my hands. Then I scared myself
by looking in the mirror.

My hair looked like it hadn't seen a comb in
weeks, my face was pale, and there was a large purple
bruise along my jawline. A small, red cut was near my
left eyebrow, and I saw the top of a bruise under the
neckline of the gown. It seemed to be a mark from
the seatbelt. My left wrist was in a soft brace from the
sprain and the skin inside it itched like there were ants
on patrol in there.

I heard the door to my room open and click shut
so I called out, "I'm in here."

I didn't want the nurse or Claire to think
something happened to me.

The door to the bathroom was practically ripped
off its hinges seconds later. The sudden action scared
me and I jumped. My weight transferred onto the IV
pole, which was on wheels, and unable to catch my
footing, I went sliding backward toward the toilet.

"What the fuck are you doing?" someone
growled in a tone that was sooo not the nurse or
Claire.

"Gavin?" I gasped.

He came forward, catching me around the waist and swinging me up into his arms.

"What are *you* doing?" I demanded.

"Stopping you from falling and killing yourself."

"Oh, please," I muttered. "Put me down. I want to walk."

"No."

"How dare you argue with a woman in the hospital!" I snapped.

"You're the only one who's arguing."

I gave him an evil look. "You're pulling on my IV."

He set me down but kept a hold on my arm like I was helpless and couldn't walk.

I opened my mouth to tell him what I thought of being treated like a ninety-year-old lady, but he narrowed his eyes. "Don't you sass me. I'll smack that fine, bare ass."

I gasped and reached around to close the back of the gown.

He smirked. "Ain't nothing I haven't seen before," he leaned down and whispered in my ear.

Memories of all the times he'd seen my naked body burned through my veins. "I need to get some clothes," I muttered.

"Claire's out in the hall, flirting with Stitch."

"Some friend she is!" I said without heat. In truth, it was nice to see her flirting. It was something she so rarely did.

I made my way back to bed. Gavin matched my slow, small steps the whole way and never complained. He didn't support me, which I would have hated, but he did stand close so that if I needed him he was there.

The aroma of baked goods and coffee wafted toward me and my stomach practically attacked my abdomen to get out. There was a brown paper sack and a couple of coffee cups sitting beside the bed.

I looked at Gavin. He was still dressed in the same clothes he wore last night. His hair was still a wreck and his clothes were more wrinkled than before.

"You haven't been home?" I said, surprised.

"No."

"You were gone when I woke up. I just assumed—"

"I went to get some decent coffee and some food. I thought you might be hungry."

I paused beside the bed. "You stayed here? All night?"

"Yes." He nudged me into the bed and then pulled the covers around my legs.

"But why?"

The door opened and Claire breezed in, looking a little bright-eyed. *Flirting must really agree with her.* "Hey, Claire."

"Hey," she said, carrying a bag of what I hoped was clothes and a hairbrush in one hand and a coffee in the other. "Thanks for the latte, Gavin."

"Anytime," he replied, handing me a tall, white cup with a lid. "Here, don't burn yourself."

"Thank you."

He pushed the chair closer to Claire and motioned for her to sit as he pulled a giant blueberry muffin out of the bag and handed it to me.

"Mmmm. That looks so good," I said, ready to devour it.

"Well, it isn't a snack cake."

I rolled my eyes. "No, this actually has fruit in it."

"Overrated."

I giggled as he picked up his own cup and took a drink. He made no effort to move away from the bed. Claire was looking between us with surprise on her face.

"What the hell is up with you two?" she said. "Are you *dating?*"

"No!" I said swiftly, feeling my cheeks burn. I gave Claire a *what the hell* look and hoped she took the hint.

"We're just friends. Gavin is Aunt Ruth's neighbor."

She looked like she wanted to argue, but I gave her the death stare and she shut up.

Thank God.

Gavin just stood there, drinking his coffee, but I was too chicken to brave a glance in his direction.

"Are those clothes for me?" I asked, motioning to the bag on the floor beside her.

"Of course."

"I want a shower so bad," I said longingly.

"Stitch said he could spring you today," Claire said.

The door to my room opened and Joanna breezed in looking like her usual perfect self. She was dressed in a pair of navy linen sailor pants and a white fitted top with ruffles at the neck. Her hair wasn't down, but swept up into a neat twist on her head. On her feet was a pair of cork wedges that accentuated her willowy height.

"Talie…" She began, breathless. "We've been so worried."

"Joanna," I said, "I'm surprised to see you." I glanced at Claire.

"I didn't know how badly you were hurt when I got here." She shrugged.

"I don't know why you would be surprised. We got up and drove first thing this morning."

"We?" I looked behind her.

"Momma, Daddy, and Jack are here, of course. They're parking the car."

They were all here? *Oh boy.*

"You didn't have to drive this whole way," I said, wishing they hadn't. I loved my family, I loved them a lot, but I really didn't want them here. Not now.

"It's only two hours," she said. "We would have been here sooner, but Jack had some important meeting yesterday he just couldn't get out of."

Beside me, Gavin shifted, and Joanna's eyes snapped to him like he was some criminal in a police lineup. "Who's this?"

"Joanna, this is Gavin. He pulled me out of the car after the accident."

"But that was days ago. Why is he still here?"

I sighed loudly. "He has ears, you know."

"Please forgive me," she said, contrite. "I'm so upset at seeing my sister this way."

"Not a problem," Gavin drawled.

"Blake should be here later today," Joanna told me.

"Why would you call him?" I asked, anxiety spiking in my chest. The last thing I wanted was another fight with him.

"He's your husband."

Beside me, Gavin stiffened.

"Soon-to-be *ex*," I said tightly.

Joanna looked between me and Gavin, her eyes calculating. I spoke, drawing away her attention. "Call Blake and tell him not to come. He isn't welcome."

"Talie," Joanna said.

I knew that tone of voice. I wasn't going to be swayed this time.

"Now, Joanna," I snapped. "I don't want him here and we are *not* getting back together."

She was taken aback by my bitchiness. She looked at Gavin like it was his fault.

Claire knew things were about to get ugly, so she wrapped an arm around Joanna and said, "Why don't we step outside and you can make that call?"

Joanna went with her, glancing back at us only once.

When the door closed behind them, I let out a sigh.

"She's a piece of work," Gavin drawled.

"She's my sister," I said simply.

"Your room's about to get real crowded, so I'll just leave you to your company."

As much as I hated it, he was right. "Thanks for staying... and for breakfast."

He leaned down, placing his hands on either side of my hips. I lifted my chin to look up into his blue eyes.

"I'm not leaving," he whispered.

"No?"

He shook his head. "I'm going to go find Stitch. Maybe bug the nurses."

I opened my mouth to ask him why he was staying, but he didn't allow me to speak. His kiss cut off any reply I would have made.

Slow burn.

That's how I would describe that kiss. It was slow and gentle, but it started this burn in my lower belly, a burn that I knew had potential to ignite into a full-on fire. When he pulled back, he pressed another kiss to my forehead and then walked away.

When he reached the door, I noticed our kiss had an audience. My parents, sister, and Jack were all standing there with mouths slack with shock. Gavin inclined his chin to my father on his way out, leaving me alone.

The rat.

My family came forward, firing a million questions at me.

It was going to be a long morning.

30

Talie

Four hours of hovering. I never knew four hours
could feel like an entire lifetime. I avoided many of
their questions by holding a hand to my head and
pretending I didn't feel well. It wasn't that much of a
lie. I did have a headache and my body was sore.

After I finished my breakfast, the nurse bustled
in and removed the IV. I was so glad to get that thing
out of my hand. I further delayed conversation about
what they walked in on between Gavin and me by
rushing off to the bathroom with the bag of clothes
Claire brought.

I didn't get away alone, though. My mother
followed me into the bathroom with a concerned
look across her features. I didn't have the heart to
kick her out of the room. Plus, she was my mom and
I kinda needed my mom right now.

The clothes Claire brought me were totally cute.
Working in a trendy department store obviously
taught her a lot about style. She brought me navy
ankle-length leggings and a kelly-green button-down

top that was loose fitting and comfy over my bruises. Beneath it went a thick white tank top, and she added a long, navy-colored necklace with a ship anchor-shaped pendant. She even brought me a pair of kelly-green sandals to match.

By the time I was dressed, I felt exhausted. Talk about pathetic. My mother must have seen it written on my face because she ordered me to sit on the toilet so she could brush my hair.

"You cut your hair," she said.

"I needed a change."

"I like it."

"You do?" I asked, surprised.

"Yes, your long hair was nice, but this suits you much better."

"Joanna told me to wear it long."

Mom leaned down. "Joanna can be a bit bossy."

I laughed.

She continued brushing, the action rather soothing. "You've been through a lot these past few weeks," she said lightly.

"I can't stay with him, Mom. He cheated on me. He told me he was going to do it again. He doesn't want a wife. He wants a trophy."

She kept brushing.

"And I got fired from my job," I admitted. "The head of the practice is a real douchebag."

"What's a douchebag?" she asked, pausing.

I stifled a laugh. "He wanted me to sleep with him as part of my job."

"You're right. He is a douchebag."

This time I couldn't keep the laugh inside me.

"Blake would never have made you happy. I've always known that." Her words were flippant, almost casual.

I looked up sharply, surprise bursting through my middle. "Really? Why didn't you say something before?"

"Sometimes we have to make our own mistakes."

"You're not upset that I'm divorcing him?" I honestly thought my mother's reaction would be just like Joanna's. I know I was a grown adult, but the opinion of my mother still mattered to me.

"I'd be upset if you didn't. You deserve better than a douchebag like him." She sniffed.

Oh boy. I think she just found a new favorite word.

"What about Daddy?" I asked, biting my lip.

"Your father wants you to be happy. Just like I do." She said it like it was common knowledge. Had I really spent all these years being so hard on myself because I thought they were all silently judging me, when really, the only one judging me had been me?

"Joanna…"

The brush paused over my head and Mom drew back to look at me. "Joanna isn't your mother. Sometimes she likes to pretend she is, but she isn't. She's your sister and she loves you, but she doesn't get a vote on how you live your life."

A heavy weight lifted off my shoulders. "I love you, Mom."

She smiled and set aside the brush. "I love you too, Talie."

From the shopping bag, she produced a hair tie and a thin, navy-colored headband. "I think off your face today. Yes?"

I nodded and she began making a small ponytail at the base of my neck.

"About that boy…"

"He's not a boy." I sighed. "And his name is Gavin."

"There's some sparks there?"

"I didn't mean for it to happen."

"Sparks like that can't be controlled, Talie."

I glanced up at her again, surprised.

"What?" she raised her eyebrows at me. "I was your age once."

"You and dad?"

She smiled.

"Gross."

"You asked."

"Ugh," I said, but inside I was actually charmed. I was glad to know my mom and dad had been married for over twenty years because they truly loved each other.

"There," she said, adding the headband to my head and admiring her work. "Beautiful."

Tears sprang to my eyes for no good reason.

"Oh, honey," she said, wrapping her arms around me. "It'll all be okay."

"I don't know if it will," I murmured. I thought about Blake and the humiliation I felt when I saw him in bed with someone else. I thought about all the times he flat-out said or implied no one else would want me. I thought about Gavin and the way he overwhelmed me with so much desire and emotion. I thought about the baby who was barely formed inside me. Gavin never said he wanted me. In fact, he said just the opposite.

Maybe it was better this way. I shouldn't jump into a relationship while getting out of another, even if there was a child involved.

"It will, honey. Life has a way of working itself out."

I sniffled and pulled away.

"Why don't you come stay with your father and me? You can take some time to heal from the accident and look for a new job when you're ready."

I nodded. "Thanks."

I left the hospital gown on the bathroom sink and took the bag and hairbrush back into my room. Jack and Joanna were by the window, having a private conversation, and my dad was checking EPSN on the TV. Claire was doing something on her smartphone.

"Well," my mom said. "It's clear that Talie is going to be just fine. I think we should quit smothering her and go back home."

"What about Talie?" Joanna asked.

"I'll bring her home in a day or so. We can stay at Aunt Ruth's until she feels like travelling." Claire offered.

"Yeah, I'm sure I'll have to see about my car before I leave," I added, incredibly grateful for Claire.

Joanna looked like she was about to protest, but Mom interceded. "We can stop at the outlets on the way home, do a little shopping. Then we can have a nice dinner."

I owed her big time.

"Well, if you're sure," Joanna said.

I nodded, trying not to look too relieved.

Mom turned to me. "Call us when you're on your way. I'll get your room ready."

"Thanks, Mom."

After we said our good-byes, everyone began filing out of the room.

"Jack," I said, and he turned back. "Is there any way you can make this divorce happen any faster?"

I did *not* want give birth to Gavin's baby while still married to Blake.

"Maybe," he said, slipping into lawyer mode. "If he doesn't contest."

"He's not going to contest," Joanna said from the doorway. I hadn't realized she was there.

"How do you know?" I asked.

"Because when I called to tell him not to come, that tawdry assistant of his answered his private cell. I'm pretty sure she doesn't mind putting up with his... crude ways just to get his family name and prestige."

The news didn't even hurt me. It just made me incredibly sad.

"Well, if he already has another relationship, then I can likely get it pushed through in six months."

"Please, Jack."

He looked at me for long moments. I don't know what he was looking for, but he must have found it. "I'll make it happen."

"Thank you," I said, rushing forward to hug him.

My burst of affection seemed to catch him off guard, but after a moment, he returned the hug. "You're family."

When they were gone, I collapsed back in the bed. "I thought they'd never leave," I groaned.

"You and me both," Claire quipped.

"I am so ready to get out of here."

"Are you ever going to tell me what's up with you and Gavin?" she asked, folding her arms over her chest.

"Nothing."

She gave me a look.

I sighed.

"Fine. There's something, but he isn't available."

She groaned. "Is he married?"

"No. Nothing like that," I said, not wanting to tell her about Dani. I wasn't sure how he would feel about that, and I wanted to respect his wishes.

Stitch entered the room in his white coat and stylish haircut. His eyes went first to Claire, and she blushed. Perhaps I needed to press her for details.

"You ready to blow this joint?" Stitch said, giving me a smile.

"Please!"

"I'd like to look you over first, but then, yeah, I'll spring ya."

I couldn't help but glance at the door, wondering where Gavin was.

"I sent him home to shower. He was scaring the patients," Stitch said, following my gaze. "He wasn't happy, but I told him I wouldn't let him back in this room unless he was clean."

"Oh…"

"I'm sure he'll be back soon," he said, pulling his stethoscope from around his neck.

"I'll wait outside," Claire said, exiting the room.

Stitch's eyes followed her as she walked away.

"You like her." I teased.

"Shhh," he silenced, pretending like he was listening to my heartbeat, but he punctuated it with a smile.

After a general exam, he glanced at me. "I guess your head is okay?" he asked, looking at the missing bandage and combed hair.

"Uh, yeah. That bandage drove me nuts."

"Still no more cramping? Any spotting?" he asked, concerned.

"No," I said, fear prickling the back of my neck. "Should I be worried about the baby?"

He shook his head. "I don't think so. It's still so early on that I'm sure everything is fine. I would order an ultrasound, but we wouldn't be able to see much."

"You're sure I'm pregnant?"

"Your HCG levels were low, so it's very new, but yes, you are. Come back in a month, maybe a little less, and we'll do an ultrasound, make sure everything looks good, take some more blood work, et cetera."

"Are you an OB?"

He smiled. "No. I'm not a baby doctor," he quipped. "But that's my best friend's baby. I want to make sure you and it are healthy. I'll have an OB there when you come in. She can read the ultrasound and look at your blood work."

I know I only just met Stitch, but I trusted him. I was intensely glad he was looking out for my baby.

"I really appreciate it."

He smiled. "Until then, take care of yourself. Rest. Don't push your body. You just went through a serious accident."

As he spoke, Gavin entered the room.

Stitch glanced at him, then gave me a smile. "I'll go get those release papers. See you in a month."

On his way out, he stopped beside Gavin and took a deep breath. "You clean up good!"

Gavin laughed and gave him a shove out the door.

When he turned back, I couldn't help but stare. He was wearing a pair of faded jeans and a red T-shirt with the word SURF written across the front. His hair was still damp on the ends and it wasn't sticking up all over his head anymore.

"Hey," I said.

"Hey." He prowled to the bedside, his eyes inspecting every inch of my body, making it tingle with desire. "You feeling better?"

"Yeah."

His azure gaze deepened to a cobalt shade and his eyes narrowed. "Then why do you have to come back in a month?"

"Just a follow-up." I lied.

"They wouldn't schedule a follow-up for your type of injuries a month away. It would only be a week or two."

"Oh." Why the hell did he have to be a doctor? I wasn't trying to keep this pregnancy from him, but I wasn't about to spring it on him either. I felt like I needed to wait until I wasn't in the hospital. Maybe by then we would have a chance to talk. "I don't know. I'll have to ask Stitch." I tried.

"Talie," he said, a warning in his tone.

I looked away from the intensity of his gaze. "I don't want to talk about it right now."

He sat on the side of the bed, using his finger to turn my chin toward him. "There's something. Did they find something in your test results?"

I searched his eyes. I didn't know what I was looking for.

"Tell me," he urged. "The thoughts I'm having right now… Please don't do that to me."

I took a breath and whispered, "I'm pregnant."

The silence stretched on so definitively I started to think he hadn't heard.

Just like hitting the play button on a screen that had been paused, he started to move. He pulled away.

"Does he know?" he asked, his voice slightly hoarse as he paced to the other side of the room.

"Who?" I asked, confused.

"That bastard you're married to."

He thought the baby was Blake's.

I guess it wasn't a stretch for him to think that. It's likely what most people would assume. He didn't know the pregnancy hormone in my system was low and just beginning to build. He didn't know I hadn't had sex with Blake in over six months.

He didn't know this baby was his.

"No, I—"

"How could you?" he said, low, spinning around to pin me with anguished eyes.

"What?"

"How could you let him touch you like that? How could you let him tie you together for the rest of your life?"

"Gavin," I said, wanting to tell him I wasn't tied to Blake. I was tied to him. The pain I saw in his eyes surprised me. It was almost like he wished this baby was his.

The door opened and Claire breezed in. "Guess who has release papers!"

Gavin and I both looked up at her. She froze. "Did I interrupt?"

"Yes," I said at the same time he said, "No."

I cleared my throat. "We were talking. Can we have another minute?"

"Sure—"

"It's not necessary," Gavin said. "We're done here."

"Gavin, wait!" I called, but it was too late. He was gone.

31

Talie

The drive to Aunt Ruth's seemed to take forever,
just like the wheelchair trip down to the car at the
hospital. They wouldn't let me walk, and I wasn't
about to make a scene, so I sat there while they
pushed me to the car.

Claire knew I was upset, but she didn't press, and
I was grateful. I wasn't ready to talk about this with
anyone. I just wanted to find Gavin. I wanted to make
him listen to me. If, after he heard this baby was
actually his, he still wanted to run, I wouldn't stop
him.

Gavin's car was in the driveway at his house. As
soon as Claire parked, I got out of the car and went
down onto the beach and up onto his deck. I knocked
on the glass sliders, but he never came to the door. I
peered into the windows, searching for him and even
called out his name, but still he didn't answer.

I spun around with a frustrated sound and
looked down on the beach. In the distance, I could

see him, a guy in jeans and red T-shirt. He was wearing a hat, but I would know him anywhere.

He was walking along the shoreline, toward the house.

I didn't think it would be a good idea to go running off down the beach after just getting released from the hospital (though I wanted to) so instead, I sat down in one of his deck chairs, willing to wait it out.

When Gavin got close, I knew he saw me because he stopped walking and stared up to where I was sitting. I stood as my heart bounced around and my hands quivered. I was afraid he might keep walking, that he might turn away again.

Instead, he started walking again, his long strides bringing him onto the deck.

"What are you doing here, Talie?" he asked.

"The baby isn't Blake's," I said loudly, over the rumbling of the waves. "It's yours."

He stilled as if shock rendered him motionless. I gave him time to process, to make sense of what I said.

"That baby isn't mine," he said, pointing to my stomach. "It's too early."

"Which is exactly why I have to go back in a month. Because an ultrasound wouldn't show anything. A blood test confirmed it."

He still looked like he didn't want to believe.

"I haven't had sex with Blake in over six months."

His eyes snapped to mine. I saw the hope there. He desperately wanted to believe. I nodded. "This baby is yours. Call Stitch. He'll tell you how early I am."

He shot forward so suddenly that I stumbled. But it didn't matter because his arms were around me in seconds, pulling me against his body and claiming my mouth with his. I was gasoline and he was the match. We burst into flames that burned brighter than the sun. His mouth was demanding as he kissed me so deeply I had to cling to his biceps to hold myself in place.

Gavin's tongue knew exactly where to stroke, the exact amount of pressure to apply, and exactly how to twist around mine. I groaned, fisting my hands in the fabric of his shirt, trying to get closer. I would climb inside him if he let me. There was no place that was close enough to him.

He broke the kiss just as suddenly as it started. His eyes looked like blue fire as he speared me with a look. "Six months?" he demanded.

I shook my head. "He hasn't touched me in six months."

He growled deep in his chest, the sound of an alpha male claiming what was his. He lifted me off my feet and carried me into the house, not stopping at the couch or against the wall like we usually did.

Instead, he carried me into his bedroom, into a room I hadn't been before. The shades were drawn so it was dim and all I could make out was a large bed in the center of the room. Gavin placed me in the center of the mattress and stood at the foot of the bed, staring down at me possessively.

With one hand, he yanked the shirt off his head and sent it flying backward, and then he reached for the button on his jeans. I pushed up to sit, scooting closer to where he stood. I climbed to my knees and pushed his hand away, reaching into the worn fabric of his jeans to cup the already rigid length inside.

In one swift movement, Gavin pushed down his jeans and boxers, leaving him completely bare and at my eye level. His cock was swollen and proud, impatient for pleasure.

I wrapped my hand around him and squeezed, rubbing my lip over his head. He made a guttural sound and I smiled, liking the power I suddenly had over him. Keeping my hand on him, I lowered down, deep-throating him in one long stroke. His body jerked like he'd been shot and his hands reached out to grip my shoulders.

I began to bob up and down on his length, using the moist heat in my mouth to make him slick. When his member began to quiver, I pulled back, licking down his length and drawing the delicate skin of his balls between my lips.

He whispered my name, but it was barely decipherable. Gavin yanked out my ponytail and headband to delve his hands into my hair. I flinched a little when he bumped the knot on the back of my head, but I ignored the sting of pain.

I tried to go at him a little more fiercely with my mouth, but he wouldn't let me, pulling me back while breathing hard.

He made short work of my clothes, throwing them places I didn't even look. All my attention was on him and his hands, on only the pleasure he could give me. When I was at last completely naked, we backed up on the bed, Gavin coming over me, making me feel small as his body blocked out everything else in the room.

He leaned down and kissed me, the kind of kiss that branded me forever his. Gavin's lips trailed down my neck and across my shoulder, sucking and licking as he went.

"I don't want anyone else to touch you again," he rasped, his voice low and deep.

I made a sound as his tongue flicked over my puckered nipple. He pulled the flesh into his mouth and rolled it around. The action felt so insanely good that I groaned and delved my fingers into his hair.

He rose over me and settled between my legs. Our eyes connected and emotion swelled up between us. It was so intense I was almost overwhelmed. Gavin pushed into me, my slick, swollen insides yielding to his satiny, rigid cock.

I cried out as my body tightened around him, every nerve ending in my entire body on fire. I couldn't even think after that. My mind just sort of blanked because there was so much pleasure there was no room for thought. When he finally brought me to release, bright lights burst behind my eyelids and I called out his name.

We lay tangled up in the sheets together, both of us breathing hard and trying not to crash from some insane high. Now that the adrenaline was draining from my system, I could tell my body wasn't too thrilled with all the action I just participated in, but I didn't care. It felt soo damn good.

"Talie," Gavin said, resting on his side and gazing down at me.

"Hmm?"

"You have no idea the kind of shit I was going through when you told me you were pregnant."

"I tried to tell you it wasn't Blake's."

"I was beyond hearing. All I could think about was how badly I wanted that baby to be mine."

I laid a hand on his cheek. "He is yours."

"He?"

"Could be a she."

His eyes glowed and he slid a palm over my flat abdomen, like he was holding the baby who was still barely formed.

"When Dani died, I thought that part of my life died with her." He confided.

I placed my hand over his so that both of us were next to our child. "I could never take her place in your heart, Gavin," I said honestly. "I want you to know that I don't expect anything from you. And I won't keep this baby from you."

His brows drew down. "Why would you say that?" His hand moved a little so he could clutch my hip.

"I know you don't want another relationship, and I understand why. I hope you will want one with this child."

He made a choked sound. "I want this child." His fingers tightened on my skin. "I want you, too."

Hope unfolded in my chest like a badly wrapped gift. "I won't be your obligation."

He made a sound. "I wanted you before I knew about the baby. It's why I followed you that night in the rain. It's why I slept by your bedside in the hospital and harassed the nurses for the best care possible. I know I've hurt you, and I know I've done this all wrong, but I can't quit you, Talie. I don't want to."

"You said you didn't love me," I whispered, my heart crumbling into a million tiny pieces.

"I was angry and afraid. It's scary to love someone after you know what it's like to lose that love."

"The timing of all of this is so bad." I gave him a watery smile. "I'm technically still married."

"You're mine," he growled, pulling me right up against his body. "I don't care what some stupid piece of paper says."

"Jack told me he'd fast-track the divorce. I can't be married to Blake when I have this baby."

He kissed me on the forehead. "We'll make it happen."

"I don't think we should live together, not right away. What if you decide you don't like me?" I worried.

He laughed, a warm, rich sound that spread over me like butter on hot toast. "What if you don't like me?"

"You do have a terrible junk food habit."

"Woman, don't mess with a man's snacks."

I smiled. "I'm going to love you, Gavin. For the rest of my life."

He frowned. Not exactly the reaction those words should withdrawal.

"I'm not going to be an easy man to be with." He cautioned. "I'm going to be overprotective and over-watchful. Sometimes I'm moody, and I'm always going to want sex."

"I think I can handle it." I smiled, my toes curling into the blankets. Never in a million years did I think my life would ever lead me here. That a no-strings-attached tryst would end up being the best thing that would ever happen to me.

But it was.

EPILOGUE

Talie

Nine months later...

I never thought I would enjoy having to be in the hospital. And I guess I still didn't. But the reason for being here this time made it all worthwhile.

I sat impatiently waiting in the bed, this time covered with nice blankets we brought from home. I stared at the door while beneath the blanket my foot fidgeted about a mile a minute.

"She'll be here in a second, sweetheart," Gavin said from beside me.

"You should have gone with her." I worried.

"Her Uncle Stitch is with her. Besides, I wanted to stay here with you."

"I'm fine, but—"

The door opened and Stitch came in, rolling a little clear bassinet. I made an impatient sound and glared at him. "What took so long?"

"We were only gone ten minutes." He laughed. "I wanted to take her down to the lounge for a soda, but I was afraid you might send the cops."

"You can't give a newborn soda!" I said, holding out my arms for my baby.

Stitch grinned mischievously and Gavin laughed. He reached down into the bassinet and picked up a little bundle wrapped in pink. At only six pounds, she looked tiny in her daddy's arms.

"Hey there, darlin'," Gavin said to his baby girl, cradling her against his chest. She turned her face toward the sound of his voice, already familiar with it.

"Hearing test went great. She's perfectly healthy," Stitch said.

For him not being a "baby doctor," he sure had been hands-on with my entire pregnancy. So much so that we asked him to be her godfather.

It was kind of sweet to see a "lady killer" like himself finally succumb to the charms of a girl. And a tiny one at that.

Before Grace Danielle Palmer was even born, she had a line of men already wrapped around her finger. Her daddy being first, of course.

She was the most beautiful baby I had ever seen (I'm not biased at all). With a little round head, pink cheeks, and wisps of blond hair, she already looked like a beach bum. Her eyes were the same beautiful color as her daddy's.

Almost three months ago to the day, I was granted a divorce from Blake. Jack kept to his word and handled everything. Right after my accident, I stayed at Aunt Ruth's for another month before Gavin convinced me to move into his place.

So far, we liked each other pretty good.

Oh, who am I kidding? I've never been happier or loved someone more.

I rested my head against the pillow, looking up at him and his daughter, marveling in how much lighter he seemed since we met. He still mourned Danielle, but his life was no longer ruled by it. Even still, I knew a piece of his heart would always belong to her.

But I was okay with that because Gavin had enough love in his body that I got more than my share. And now Grace would too.

"I want my baby," I said, holding out my arms.

Gavin smiled down at her, then gently handed her over, placing her in my arms. "Hey, peanut," I said, and she turned toward me. Her wide, innocent eyes were incredible.

"I'll see you tomorrow?" Stitch said, looking at Gavin.

He laughed. "Not. You know I'm off rounds for the next two weeks. But feel free to stop by the beach to see your goddaughter."

He grinned and leaned over me and the baby. "Bye, Grace. I'll bring ya soda."

I rolled my eyes.

"He's a bad influence," I said when he was gone.

"He loves her."

"I know."

"I love you, Talie," he said, easing down on the bed with us. "So much."

"I love you, too."

"After Dani died, I never thought I'd be happy again. If you hadn't been so loud and annoying, I probably never would have stomped outside and fallen in love."

"Well, if you hadn't been wearing just your boxers, I probably wouldn't have fallen in love." I sniffed.

He grinned.

"So," he said casually. "I got you a present." He produced a long, velvet box and held it in front of me.

While he held it, I lifted the lid, thinking it was some sort of necklace with her birthstone.

I was wrong.

It was a diamond ring. An engagement ring. And it was lying in a bed of pink rose petals.

I gasped, more than surprised. "I thought we said we were going to wait."

Marriage had come up once or twice, but given my very recent divorce and his gun-shy feelings about getting married again, we decided we didn't have to be married to be together.

"We can have a long engagement if that's what you want," he said, watching me. "But I want you and that's never going to change. I want you to carry my name like Grace. I want people to know you're mine. Being with you is more than enough, but marrying you would be perfection."

I glanced down at Grace, giving her a little smile. "Think we should keep him?"

She made a little sound that I'm pretty sure meant she was hungry. But I took it as a yes.

"Score for Dad!" he said, rubbing a hand on her little cheek.

"Of course I'll marry you, Gavin. Nothing would make me happier."

Pink rose petals spilled across the bed as he pulled the ring out of the box and slipped the one carat solitaire onto my finger. It was shaped like a heart.

"You brought my heart back to life, Talie," he said, kissing the stone I now wore on my finger. "It's only fitting you should wear it."

So I did.

And I never took it off.

THE END

AUTHOR'S NOTE

"Writing a novel is like driving a car at night. You can see only as far as your headlights, but you can make the whole trip that way."

—*E.L. Doctorow*

Sadly, I don't know who the author who said this quote is or what they write, but when I first read it (thank you, author Julia Crane) it really struck a chord within me. That quote up there ^^^^^^^^yeah, that one^^^^^^^^ is exactly how I felt when I wrote *Tryst*. I didn't always know where the story was headed or what the plot should be, but I kept driving, and slowly, I made it home.

Many of you know that *Tryst* is actually coming to you a month late (sorry!) because when I was supposed to be writing, we moved. We didn't move states again, thank goodness. We actually only moved a few minutes away, but hey, a move is still a move, LOL. So it's been a crazy month or two for me here.

After I wrote *Tattoo* I started *Tryst* and planned on pounding it out before I moved, but it didn't really work out that way. Ha-ha. I got really busy and frankly, my brain was fried. So I took several weeks off from writing to move and set up my house. Well, when it came time to sit and write again... it was difficult.

I'm going to let you in on a little writerly secret. For writers, writing is like a drug (though, I can't speak for all writers). When you're writing a book and so in tune with the characters and the plot, you kind of slip away into your own reality. It's a thrill; it's a high. You know those guys who make your stomach flop when you read them? Or make you smile and bite your lip while you're staring at the page? Yeah, those book boys do that to the writers too. It's like experiencing your first love over and over again. So when you go without that feeling for too long, it's kind of like going through withdrawal. And for me, the more I wanted to write, the harder it became. I was jonesing for a fix but had nowhere to score one. Something like that messes with your mind. (I never said writers weren't odd!) You get into a cycle and then you think you can't write, that you've lost your mojo, that you will never get it back!

So yeah, anyway, my point is: starting a new book after taking too much time off is hell. I felt like I was floundering in the dark, trying to come up with a good plot. Finally, I told myself to get over it and sit in the chair. I did and the story came.

Talie is one of my favorite female characters. Really. I had a lot of worry about writing this book almost entirely in just her point of view. I know you guys are used to my books being dual POV. I really debated on whether or not to include Gavin's voice in the story. But the more I wrote Talie, the more she came to life. The more she shared with me about herself. I know this book is also about Gavin, but when I think of this book, I think of it as Talie's story. For me, as I was writing, her internal struggle was very profound. For some reason, she really resonated with me. I think maybe she will resonate with a lot of people. I think a lot of women find themselves looking in the mirror one day and realizing their life isn't what they thought it was. They find themselves unhappy or caring too much what other people think; they try to do what other people think is best. And then one day, they wake up and realize life's too short for all that.

And yeah, Gavin had a lot of realizations too, and his story actually brought me to tears a couple times, but I decided to leave out his POV. Why? Because I liked the mystery of Gavin. I liked seeing these little glimpses of a broken man. I liked seeing him make me swoon one second and then make me want to punch him the next. I wanted people to try and figure him out. I wanted people to be propelled through the pages, just wanting to know why he was the way he was. I felt like if I put his voice in the book, then all that would have been lost. You would have known his secrets in the beginning and you would only be reading to see what happened when Talie found out.

If you haven't figured it out... I love this book. It's one of those stories that kind of sank deep down inside me and planted itself there. It's not as action-packed as some of my other ones, and no one is trying to kill anyone... yet for me, the story was still so beautiful.

I genuinely hope that some of you readers out there get even just a little of what I said while you were reading. I hope that some of you enjoyed this book as much as I have.

Another little secret about *Tryst*... Boy, I'm just full of insight and secrets today, aren't I? Anyway, for months, this book had a different cover. This cover was done way back when the cover for *Tricks* was done. I had bookmarks and swag made. I had T-shirts made too.

And then I changed my mind.

And changed it again.

Then changed it again.

Yes. I'm serious. I'm surprised Regina Wamba of Mae I Design even wants to work with me anymore. Ha-ha-ha-ha.

The original cover is that of just a woman. Her eyes cast downward, blond hair over her shoulder. In all honesty, the truth of why I didn't use it is because I was afraid it wasn't sexy enough. I was afraid people would see the title *Tryst* and then see a woman solo on the book cover and wonder what the hell I was thinking.

I was afraid readers wouldn't pick it up as readily, and then they would miss this story.

And so as I sit here typing this just days (literally) before the cover reveal, my amazing designer is making me another cover. I haven't seen it yet. I have no doubt it will be awesome. So let's all send Regina of Mae I Design some good mojo and whisper a little thanks that she is willing to put up with my kooky behavior.

And that goes for Cassie McCown, my editor, too. She was very flexible to work with me when I needed to push the editing date back and then very flexible when I told her I needed to get this book out to all the people waiting for it.

I think this might be my longest "author's note" I've written. Ha-ha-ha. Are you still with me? If you are, *Thank You*. Thank you for reading my books, for making them a success. Thank you for waiting so patiently for *Tryst* when I know you were so anxious.

I sincerely hope it was worth the wait.

See you next book!

Cambria

P.S. I forgot to say that the reason Gavin sits around in his underwear and eats snack cakes all day is because that's what my kids said I should write about. Really. They asked me if I needed inspiration, and I said yes... That is what they came up with. So there ya go.

Turn the page for a sneak peek of
TRASHY,
the next *Take It Off* novel,
coming June 2014!

Cambria Hebert

TRASHY
Sneak Peek

Roxie
High school…

The distinct sound of bowling balls cracking against pins reverberated through the entire building, echoing out the door and into the parking lot. We stood by a row of cars while a couple of the people in our group smoked the last of their cigarettes before going in to claim our lane.

I lived in a small town. Most people probably didn't even know it was on the map. It was surrounded by mountains and had just as many bars as it did churches. The economy here sucked, and it seemed like the general population was aging. The young people could be broken down into two groups:

1. Those who got stuck here and never left and

2. Those who got out and never came back

The unfortunate people who fell into group one usually worked in jobs they hated for too little pay and grew more and more bitter as they aged.

I planned on being in group two and getting the hell out of here as soon as I could. Like right after high school. There had to be more out here than this.

I'd worked hard to keep my grades up. I'd kept my nose clean and stayed away from drugs. Two more years and I could bid this town good-bye and start over, hopefully somewhere warmer.

"Can we go in?" I said. "It's freezing out here."

January in a tiny town in Maryland was one reason I would never smoke. Who wanted to stand outside in the freezing cold just to get a fix?

"Hey, we're going in!" Lena yelled, and we started up the little ramp that led inside. Lena and I had been best friends since middle school when we got randomly sat at the same table. She was outgoing and didn't seem to mind I wasn't. We became fast friends and she introduced me to her circle of friends who then, in turn, became my friends too.

Lena was the pretty one. The one who always got sidelong glances from the guys in the hallway. When a school dance was held, she always had offers, always had a date.

I was sort of invisible beside her.

Okay, people saw me. It wasn't as if I were a ghost. But I wasn't really the main attraction. No guy ever looked at me just a little too long because I'd caught his eye. Every guy I've ever crushed on thought of me like a sister or didn't know I existed. I'd never been to a school dance because no one ever asked me.

Yeah, I could go alone.

How pathetic would that be?

I pretended I didn't want to go. I pretended that school dances just weren't my thing. But they were my thing. And every time the sweetheart dance or homecoming dance would roll around, something inside me would shrink just a little because no one thought I would make a good date.

I liked to think I was waiting, that no other guy would matter until the right one came along. That the guy who noticed me first, the one who stared just a little too long… He was the one who mattered. He was the one who deserved my heart.

Besides, falling in love in this town would just make my plan of getting the hell out even harder. I wanted love. I wanted to see that look in someone's eye. You know, the look where you are their entire world.

But I wanted out of here more.

Inside, the bowling alley was packed. If we hadn't reserved a lane for cyber bowling, we wouldn't have gotten one. Cyber bowling was one of the town's only things to do here on the weekend besides get drunk and party at someone's house whose parents weren't home.

And we did plenty of that.

But sometimes we wanted to get out. To see and be seen.

Bowling at midnight on a Friday, with nothing but black lights, flashing strobe lights, and a blaring jukebox was the way to do it.

Yes. I found it extremely ironic that we went out to see and be seen in a bowling alley where they shut off all the lights.

There used to be a club, a teen club, just fifteen minutes up the road. It was the kind of place we couldn't go to without our male friends. Because a group of girls there alone was ripe for the picking. Your ass got grabbed; you got propositioned; you got leered at. One time I got hauled onto the dance floor by some drunk guy (who likely was not a teenager) who locked his arms around me and refused to let go.

I'm pretty sure he wasn't the guy I've been waiting for all my life.

Gross.

"You know you want these," Lena said, handing over a pair of ass-ugly brown loafers that Velcro-ed closed.

"Girl, I am going to rock these," I quipped and strutted over to our lane.

She laughed and followed along. A couple guys a few lanes away whistled at her.

Lena had long, thick blond hair, curves that probably made her daddy crazy, and a laugh that made you think she had quite a bit of naughty under all that nice.

I had plain brown hair, plain brown eyes, and the only curves I had were from the cell phone in the back pocket of my jeans.

"Did we get two lanes?" I asked, glancing at the one right beside ours. It was empty too.

"Christy invited her boyfriend. He's bringing his friends," Lena said, strapping on her ugly shoes.

Christy was another friend of ours. She was dating a senior at the other high school here in this town. I'd seen him around but never really talked to him. My stomach felt a little funny over a whole lane of guys we didn't know next to us all night. Not that it mattered. They would all fall over Lena when they saw her.

The rest of our friends filtered in from the cold, and we all stood around laughing and poking fun at each other and our ugly feet. Christy was sitting on her boyfriend's lap when several guys walked up. Kevin (Christy's boyfriend) stood up and gave them all high-fives and fist-bumps.

I swear cavemen probably did the same thing back in the day when they clubbed their dinner and dragged it home.

I turned away and started entering names into the screens overhead, the one that kept our scores. Bowling started in like five minutes and someone had to do this. After I filled out our lane's menu, I switched over to Kevin's, typing his name in first.

Lena came up beside me, a guy right behind her. "This is Ben," she said.

I gave him a wave and typed his name in.

"There is also a PJ, Chris, and…" Lena's voice trailed off as she was looking toward the group of guys, trying to see who else was here.

"I don't know the other guy's name," she whispered.

Ben had already wandered off to find a ball.

"He can type it in," I said and spun around to step away from the computer.

"It's Craig," a low voice whispered in my ear.

His breath feathered over my ear, causing my eyes to droop just a little. Goose bumps raced down my spine and filled my toes, making them tingle.

I turned to glance over my shoulder.

He had blue eyes.

He was still incredibly close.

"What?" I said, unable to look away.

"My name," he said, giving me a half smile. "For the screen." He motioned to it, reminding me it was there.

"Oh," I said. "Right."

He grinned. He had a dimple on each side of his mouth. Broad shoulders. Full lips. And a backward baseball cap pulled over his forehead.

I was staring.

I couldn't not stare at him.

"You any good at bowling?" he asked.

How had I not seen him around before? Where the hell had he been?

"The best," I said. "I always win."

He flashed a grin. "Not tonight. I don't lose. Especially to a girl."

Is he flirting with me?

"Roxie," Lena called, stepping up to my side. "You're up."

This was the part where I would lose his attention. This was the part where he saw he had better options.

He gave Lena the *what up* gesture with his chin.

He kept his eyes on me.

He kept his eyes on me.

I smiled. "I hope your ego can handle it when you lose tonight. Especially to a girl," I told him.

"Game on," he said, backing toward his lane. Not once did he look away.

Butterflies lifted their wings and took flight in my belly.

Lena pulled me away and shoved me near the thingy that returned your ball. Cool air blew up from the vent, causing a few strands of my hair to float out around me.

"You know him?" she whispered.

"No. Do you?" I whispered back.

"Just that he's a friend of Kevin's."

I nodded. I didn't tell her how hot I thought he was. I didn't mention the freaking butterfly sanctuary inside my middle. I calmly picked up the ball I was going to use and walked toward the center dot on the approach.

I would be silly to mention it when I knew he probably wasn't interested.

Before I overthought it, I stole a glance over my shoulder. He was sitting in the chairs, laughing at something one of the guys said. His dimples were on full display.

But even though he was having a conversation with them, he was still looking at me.

I looked away. A little thrill of something shot through me. I stared down at the pins, barely even registering them.

Maybe he's the one you've been waiting for, my heart whispered.

I couldn't have been more wrong.

Cambria Hebert is the author of the young adult paranormal *Heven and Hell* series, the new adult *Death Escorts* series, and the new adult *Take it Off* series. She loves a caramel latte, hates math, and is afraid of chickens (yes, chickens). She went to college for a bachelor's degree, couldn't pick a major, and ended up with a degree in cosmetology. So rest assured her characters will always have good hair. She currently lives in North Carolina with her husband and children (both human and furry), where she is plotting her next book. You can find out more about Cambria and her work by visiting http://www.cambriahebert.com.